US

STO

FRIENDS
OF ACPL

P9-EFJ-175

X

LUCKY SEVEN

Books by Matt Christopher

LUCKY SEVEN

Sports Stories by Matt Christopher

Illustrated by Harvey Kidder

BOSTON · Little, Brown and Company · TORONTO

COPYRIGHT © 1970 BY MATTHEW F. CHRISTOPHER

ALL RIGHTS RESERVED. NO PART OF THIS BOOK MAY BE REPRODUCED IN
ANY FORM OR BY ANY ELECTRONIC OR MECHANICAL MEANS INCLUDING
INFORMATION STORAGE AND RETRIEVAL SYSTEMS WITHOUT PERMISSION IN
WRITING FROM THE PUBLISHER, EXCEPT BY A REVIEWER WHO MAY QUOTE
BRIEF PASSAGES IN A REVIEW.

LIBRARY OF CONGRESS CATALOG CARD NO. 75-108169

THIRD PRINTING

Many of the stories in this book originally appeared in magazines, and the author is grateful to the following for permission to reprint material first published by them:

The Westminster Press for "The Reluctant End," published in *Trailblazer*, October 24, 1965, © 1965 by W. L. Jenkins; and for "Stop That Puck!," published in *Trailblazer*, November 20, 1966, © 1966 by W. L. Jenkins.

The Light and Life Press for "Bunt That Ball!," published in *Story Trails*, May 29, 1955.

Straight magazine for "Baseballs and Bumblebees," published in *Straight*, June 3, 1962. © 1962 by the Standard Publishing Company.

The Sunday School Board of the Southern Baptist Convention for "No Spot for Jerry," published in *Adventure*, April 14, 1963. © Copyright 1963, The Sunday School Board of the Southern Baptist Convention. Used by permission.

The Society of the Divine Savior for "Substitute Sophomore," published in *Manna*, June, 1953.

*Published simultaneously in Canada
by Little, Brown & Company (Canada) Limited*

PRINTED IN THE UNITED STATES OF AMERICA

U. S. 1930513

To my sons
Marty, Dale and Duane

Publisher's Note

Matt Christopher's sports novels have established themselves as favorites of young readers searching for stories that will help them understand something about themselves as well as provide fast-paced action. These same readers have never had a chance to read Mr. Christopher's shorter fiction in book form. We are happy to correct this oversight in publishing this volume.

Of the seven stories included here, two are somewhat of a departure for the author. With "Full Throttle" he leaves the area of team sports to deal with the fierce competition that has grown up around the pastime of slot car racing, and "Baseballs and Bumblebees" shows the author mining a more humorous vein than he normally uses.

We hope that *Lucky Seven* will be a satisfying experience for all those young people who clamor for more of a good thing.

Contents

The Reluctant End

RUSTY stared at the blank wall. All his hopes of beating the powerful Bearcats were suddenly shattered. Sadly he placed the phone back onto its hook, Coach Pearson's words still humming in his ears.

Rollie Pike sick with the flu! The best receiver the Warhawks had, and he had to come down with the flu!

But that wasn't the worst of it. The coach had asked him, Rusty, if he'd play left end in Rollie's place tomorrow.

He had never played end in his life!

Who did the coach intend to play quarterback? Eddie Krantz? That little, half-pint southpaw? That second-stringer? He could run like a rabbit, but he didn't know much about football.

Well, the Warhawks might as well hand the game over to the Bearcats. With Rollie in there they would have stood a good chance of winning. With Rollie out, it would be murder. Just plain murder.

Rusty hadn't told Coach Pearson that he had no desire to play in Rollie's place, but that's how he felt about it.

"You're tall and you have a good pair of hands, Rusty," the coach had said to him over the phone. "That's why I think you'd be the best guy to put in Rollie's place."

Tall, and a good pair of hands. They were nice, kind words, all right. But if you didn't have a passer, what good would being tall and having a good pair of hands do? Nothing, that's what.

Rusty got off the chair and walked glumly away from the phone, hoping that Mom or Dad wouldn't see the depressed look on his face. They'd know something was wrong for sure.

When the game started at one o'clock the next day, a warm, sunny Saturday afternoon, Eddie Krantz was in the safety slot. He was hardly taller than Tom Thumb, but he had gumption. You had to give him credit for that.

The Bearcats kicked off and Beans Jackson, the Warhawks' gangly right halfback, caught the ball and ran it back to his own thirty-three before he was tackled.

In the huddle, Eddie called a play for Bruce Fazio, the fullback, to carry the ball.

"Get set! One! Two! Hike!" Eddie's tinny voice sounded like BB shots.

Fats Munro, the center, snapped the ball. Eddie grabbed it in his small hands, stepped back, turned and handed off to Bruce. Bruce plunged over their left tackle for a two-yard gain.

In the horseshoe huddle little Eddie crouched in front of them with his elbows on his knees and his eyes peering intently over the nose guard of his helmet. It didn't seem right to Rusty that Eddie was standing there, calling the plays, commanding the situation as if he had done the job hundreds of times before.

It just isn't fair, thought Rusty. He knows nothing about football. I know ten times as much as he does.

"Let's try Play Twenty-one," murmured Eddie, not too confidently.

"Twenty-one?" The words popped out of Rusty's mouth before he could stop them. "Why don't you have Bruce or somebody run it again? We don't want to try a pass *yet!*"

Eddie's brown eyes swung to him. Bewilderment filled them for a moment.

"Oh, let him call the plays, Rusty," said Fats. "He's quarterback now."

"Right," said right end Dutch Ferguson. Several nodding heads indicated that the majority went along with Fats.

Rusty shrugged, his face turning pink. He was glad that his face was in shadow and no one could see him blush.

Play Twenty-one was the favorite pass play Rusty used when the Warhawks really needed to gain ground. It didn't always work, but most of the time it did — when *he* called it and when Rollie Pike was receiving.

It just wouldn't work now. Rusty was sure of that. Eddie simply couldn't throw a football hard enough to make a long pass work.

The team broke out of the huddle, got into formation, and Eddie began barking signals. At the snap he took the ball, faded back, faked a handoff to Bruce, then heaved the pass to Rusty who was running down toward the left side of the field — running slowly, so he'd be sure to catch Eddie's weak pass.

Horror struck him. The ball was sailing high! He stepped up his pace, but it was too late. The ball soared over his head and hit the ground.

"What did you slow down for?" Bruce shouted at him as they assembled again into a huddle.

"I didn't think he could —!" Rusty didn't finish what he was going to say. He felt his face flush again, for the second time in less than a minute.

Eddie called for a repeat of the play, but

this time Rusty was covered like a tent. Eddie, stumped as to what to do with the ball, was smothered behind the line of scrimmage for a big loss. On the next play they lost the ball to the Bearcats.

Craig Alo, the Bearcats' fleet-footed full-back, carried the ball twice for a first down, bringing the ball to the Warhawks' eight-yard line.

Tension mounted as the Warhawks tried to form a strong wall to stop the Bearcats from scoring a touchdown. The end zone was well covered for an aerial attack. Rusty and Beans were prepared for a wide, end-around run.

The signals were called and the center snapped the ball.

A quick pass over center! The halfback caught it, sidestepped Bruce, and plunged over for a touchdown.

A few seconds later the Bearcats split the uprights and went into the lead, 7 to 0.

Dismay overwhelmed the Warhawks. There they were, heading for another loss.

It was Rusty who tried to pepper them up.

This was something he had learned to do — to instill courage into the guys when they fell behind. Quarterback or not — discouraged as he was about playing end — he was still a member of the team. He still had to give all he had, and he asked the team to give too.

His encouraging cries helped, but not enough. The Bearcats came through with two more touchdowns — one on a fourteen-yard pass, the other on a fifty-six yard run by Craig Alo.

In the second half, after a great return by Beans, Bruce ran for eighteen yards to get the pigskin on the Bearcats' nine-yard line. Eddie called for Play Twenty-one again in a desperate attempt to score against the tough, powerful Cats.

The throw was good. But the ball struck Rusty's fingers, glanced off, and bounced to the ground.

"Rusty!" Bruce yelled.

Once again Rusty's face turned color — a bright red now, not pink.

Coach Pearson's words echoed and re-

© 1922 04442 7919

echoed in his ears. *You're tall and you have a good pair of hands. That's why I think you'd be the best guy to put in Rollie's place.*

Well, he won't think that anymore, thought Rusty. I've proved to him that being tall and having a good pair of hands don't make a good pass receiver. It takes more than that, and I don't have it.

The game ended with the Bearcats running over the Warhawks by a score of 27 to 0. It was a slaughter. Rusty realized that it need not have been so. The Bearcats could have had two touchdowns, but Rusty had eased up on his running, and he had missed that pass.

You couldn't blame that on Eddie Krantz!

The week went by dismally. The Warhawks had practice Tuesday through Thursday and rest on Friday so that they would be well prepared for their game against the Gray Foxes on Saturday.

It was a sad week for Rusty. In school, some of the guys seemed less friendly toward him than usual. Not all of them, of course. Bruce,

Fats, Beans — most of them acted as though the game last week had never happened.

Eddie was rather quiet. But then he was always quiet. He knew he had a tinny voice, and he tried not to use it unless he really had to.

"I'll talk more when my voice changes," he had said once. The guys had laughed. No matter what, you just had to like Eddie. He was that kind of a kid.

At practice, Coach Pearson had Rusty running all over the field catching passes. Some he caught easily; some he couldn't.

I wonder if he expects to turn me into a great pass receiver in one week, Rusty reflected. He hoped Rollie Pike would be well enough to play Saturday. Surely he should be okay by then.

But Rollie wasn't. He had gotten over the flu, but the doctor had said he had better rest a few more days before indulging in any activities. Man, what awful luck!

So Eddie played in the quarterback slot again in the game against the Gray Foxes and

Rusty played left end. Rusty's feelings about the matter weren't any different from before. He still wanted the quarterback position; he still preferred calling the plays and barking the signals. There was more ball handling, more excitement in the quarterback spot.

He tried to put these thoughts out of his mind. He'd try to play left end as the Coach had suggested. He'd play the best he could.

The Gray Foxes, in red and gray uniforms, won the call when the coin was flipped. They chose to receive. Within two minutes they pulled down a forward pass that netted forty-two yards. On the next play, their right half-back, Pete Sanders, plunged over for the touchdown. Fats blocked the kick for the extra point and the Gray Foxes led, 6 to 0.

Beans caught the kickoff and raced to the Gray Foxes' twenty-eight-yard line before being pulled down. Eddie called for a jump pass to Dutch Ferguson down the right side of the field. It netted six yards. Bruce picked up another two on a line plunge through left tackle, and then Eddie plowed through for a first down on a sneak. He just made it, but it was enough.

The ball was spotted on the Gray Foxes' eighteen-yard line. Eighteen more yards and the score would be tied. A conversion would put the Warhawks ahead.

"Twenty-two!" said Eddie in the huddle.

All faces turned in unison to Dutch. The pass was to him this time. *Let's make it good!* their looks pleaded.

It was a long pass. Dutch was running out into the end zone, trying to catch it.

Suddenly a pair of hands reached up, pulled the ball down, and the runner took off with it into the opposite direction!

An interception! The Gray Fox player ran down the field without interference. Not a Warhawk was in his way. He went the entire distance for a touchdown. This time the conversion was good and the score widened to 13–0.

Rusty thought that Eddie's pass should have

been higher, but he said nothing. On two occasions last week he had opened his mouth and put his foot into it. He didn't want that to happen again.

In the second half, the Gray Foxes rolled again. They got the ball on the Warhawks' twenty-one — then fumbled! Eric Schmidt, subbing for Bruce Fazio, recovered for the Warhawks.

In three plays the Warhawks gained a first down. And Eddie called for Play Twenty-one.

Now all eyes turned briefly to Rusty. They pleaded again, *Let's make it good!*

Eddie barked signals in his tinny voice. The ball was snapped. Eddie faked off to Bruce, then faded back. Down the field, on the left side, Rusty was running hard.

Eddie let the ball fly. It sailed through the air like a missile. Rusty reached out, caught the ball and raced on for a touchdown!

Rusty felt great as Eddie and the team jumped up and down with joy and slapped him heartily on the back and shoulders. In the melee he and Eddie shook hands. Bruce kicked for the extra point and it was good. Gray Foxes–13; Warhawks–7.

They rolled on, playing better now, with Rusty forgetting about the quarterback slot. He was an end now. Perhaps he wasn't Rollie Pike, but he was a good end who could perform when called on.

With less than a minute to go the Gray Foxes tried a pass. A long high one floated down the center of the field. Rusty started after it. It was just possible . . .

He caught it on the tips of his fingers, pulled it to him, and headed toward the Gray Foxes' goal line! Five yards . . . ten . . . fifteen . . . And then he was tackled on the Gray Foxes' twenty-one!

The Warhawks got to within four yards of the goal line when the whistle shrilled. The game was over.

It was no disgrace, though. They had done well. Much better than anyone had expected.

"Just a little more time and we would've taken them," said Bruce as they started off the field.

"I should have tried another pass to Rusty," said Eddie, his eyes shining brightly.

Rusty smiled. "Good thing you didn't. They had me covered like a blanket. But you did fine, Eddie. You know, as far as I'm concerned, you can play quarterback anytime you want — as long as I play end!"

Bunt That Ball!

"JAMIE!"

Jamie Wilcox turned at the sound of manager Ted Salin's voice. A lock of unruly, blondish hair showed under his blue baseball cap with the letter M on it, and just for a second he stopped chewing the gum in his mouth.

He stepped back toward the dugout, a bat in his hands. He crouched on one knee and looked the manager square in his level, blue eyes. "Yeah, Ted?" he said curiously.

"Look, Jamie," Ted explained. "It's the fifth inning and the score is tied. With a man on second and no outs, let's pull a surprise here. You might hit that ball, but you've got to hit it good and far to drive that man in."

"What do you want me to do?" Jamie
asked, chewing on his gum again. He couldn't
think of anything else Ted could suggest but
to plaster that ball into the next county, or at
least, over the fence.

"Get up there an' lay one down," Ted said.

Jamie paled. For a moment the freckles
around his nose stood out like copper pennies.
"Do you mean that, Ted?"

"I do, Jamie," Ted nodded. "Aim it for
third. They're playing deep. We've got to get
Castner to third. Even if you're put out,
there'll still be Steve and Johnny who might
knock him in."

"But I'm no bunter!" Jamie exclaimed. His
brows curled in disappointment. He wanted
so much to hit that ball!

Ted grinned amiably, and patted Jamie's
spiked shoe. "You can bunt as well as any of
'em, kid. Come on. Get up there."

Jamie rose and went to the plate, shaking
his head.

Outside of the batter's zone he paused,

hitched his pants and firmly tugged his cap.
He chewed harder on the gum.

Then he stepped to the plate and faced the
Blackbirds' pitcher.

The Magpies' fans whistled and applauded.
The visitors' fans welcomed him too — but
not in the same way. They hissed and booed.
It didn't bother Jamie, though. It was natural
for the opposing team's fans to put up this
same sort of exhibition every time the home
team's star slugger came to the plate.

Jamie enjoyed the fuss they made over him.
He could single out voices asking him to hit a
home run — or just to pole one out somewhere. It was what they expected of him. Lots
of them came just to see him hit. What a sad
case it would be if he let them down!

Bunt? Who ever heard of real hitters bunting? What was Ted thinking of, anyway?

"C'mon, Jamie, ol' boy! Hit that apple!"

"Drive it over that fence, Jamie!"

He stood at the plate and watched the first

pitch come in, just cutting the outside corner. He let it breeze by.

"Strike one!" called the umpire.

The next pitch came in chest-high, where he liked 'em. He stepped into it, cut viciously and heard the wood connect with a solid thud.

Loud cheers filled the warm August air as Jamie rounded first. A thin smile tugged at the corners of his lips. From what he could judge by the feel of his bat against that ball, the ol' pill was probably still going.

Then a tremendous roar exploded from the stands. Jamie, racing toward second, glanced up. The centerfielder had made a sensational catch and was heaving the white sphere back toward the infield!

Jamie's heart sank.

"Oh, you —" he said, stopping dead. He glanced at Artie Castner who had been on second. Artie had tagged up after the ball was caught and was tearing up the dirt for third. He arrived there safely. Jamie was thankful for that. At least his disobeying Ted's orders

had not made any difference. Ted had wanted
Artie to get on third, and that's where he was.

"That was a good try, Jamie," Ted Salin
said coldly as he approached the dugout. "But
I told you to bunt. Why didn't you listen
to me?"

"I guess I was trying to be smart," Jamie
answered contritely. He ducked under the
roof of the dugout and squeezed in between
Harold Jones and Petey McMinnis, second
baseman and shortstop respectively.

"Maybe this ball club's too good to have a
manager," Ted said softly.

Jamie crossed his arms and slouched down
on the bench, still chewing the gum. Why
should Ted be sore? He had advanced Artie,
hadn't he? Jamie shrugged. It was really a silly
thing to argue about, he thought.

He saw Steve Johnson get the signal from
Ted before going to the plate. Steve was a
tall, black-haired boy, usually a pretty good
sticker.

He laid the first pitch down, a perfect bunt. He dropped his bat and raced for first, while Artie Castner made a beeline for home. The Blackbirds' pitcher fielded the ball and heaved it in. Artie slid, swirling dust up and around the plate.

"Safe!" cried the man in blue.

The run broke the tie. The Magpies went ahead, 4 to 3.

Marty Abrams held the Blackbirds hitless in the next two frames and the Magpies tucked the game in the bag.

On the bus going home Marty sat with Jamie. The boys had showered and changed into street clothes and now looked fresh.

Marty said, "Ted's pretty sore you didn't listen to him. You should've seen his face when you cut at that ball instead of bunting."

"I guess I was wrong, not doing what he told me," Jamie said, looking away from the window. "But you know, yourself, it was crazy to have me bunt. I'm a hitter, not a bunter."

"It isn't that, Jamie," Marty said quietly. "Ted's manager, and he knows his stuff. He's played a lot of ball."

"Well, I won't worry about it," replied Jamie confidently, turning back to the window. "He knows he can't keep me out of a game."

"I wouldn't be so sure," Marty said.

"Well, I am," retorted Jamie stubbornly. He reached into his pocket for a fresh stick of gum, stripped the wrappings off it and poked it into his mouth.

At game time Saturday afternoon, Jamie Wilcox got the surprise of his life. Ted Salin omitted him from the lineup. Dickie Stutz, the utility outfielder, was in his place.

"How come I'm not playing, Ted?" Jamie asked the manager after gathering the nerve to approach him. Jamie just couldn't figure it. He was the Magpie's big gun at the plate.

Ted's blue eyes met his. His jaw squared. "I'm manager of this ball team, Jamie. When the season started every one of you asked me if I'd take the job. I said I'd be glad to, on the condition that nobody disputed my orders. You were one of the strongest in supporting that condition. Then last Thursday you hit when I told you to bunt. You've been playing good ball all season. All of you have, or we wouldn't be fighting for the pennant. But you've got the idea in your head that you're the star of the team, that you can do what you want. I don't want that, Jamie. I don't want any stars. I just want a good, fighting ball club with each man doing the best he can. A team that plays together and takes orders when I think they should be given."

He paused, as if waiting to see whether Jamie might have something to say. Jamie didn't. There were too many things to think about.

Jamie knew suddenly that Ted was right. Everything Ted said hit home. He truly hadn't realized that the ball club had come pretty far since the season had started, and the reason for the players' success had a lot to do with the way Ted had managed them.

"Guess maybe you're right, Ted," Jamie finally said, the words barely squeezing past the lump in his throat.

He turned and went to the dugout, feeling Ted's look boring into his back. He half-hoped Ted might change his mind, but when the game started against the Bluejays Dickie Stutz was playing left field.

The game got a slow start. Neither team scored until the third, when the lead-off man for the Magpies, Harold Jones, banged a double, followed by three singles in a row by Petey, Artie, and Steve Johnson. Steve was batting clean-up today.

The game ended with the lopsided score: Magpies 11, Bluejays 3.

Jamie, on the bench, had never suffered through a longer game in his life.

The win placed the Magpies one game away from the pennant. It was now between them and the Catbirds, the only other team who had suffered just one defeat all season.

The final game pitted the two top contenders and was played on a neutral diamond. What a terrible surprise it was to Jamie when he discovered that again Ted Salin had left him out of the lineup.

He felt deeply hurt. Was Ted deliberately humiliating him in front of the team? And this — the big game of the year!

He tried to be reasonable about it. Maybe Ted was right in doing this. Maybe Ted meant to show that a manager was there for a definite purpose and orders were given to be obeyed.

The game got under way. Marty Abrams, on the mound for the Magpies, shot the ball in like a bullet and kept the Catbirds scoreless for the first two innings. In the bottom of the second Johnny Myers, the Magpies' fleet-footed centerfielder, banged out a single. Kenny Schatz walked. Danny Myers, Johnny's tow-headed brother, connected with a terrific double that brought in two runs. In the next inning they scored two more on errors.

The fans went wild. The only person who felt glum was Jamie Wilcox, who sat with his arms crossed and chewed gum very slowly.

Something surprising happened in the top of the third. It was as if the Catbirds had been playing possum all this while. They got to Marty and started hitting him all over the lot. No matter what he threw, they hit it.

Ted took Marty out while they were still ahead, 4 to 3.

Bernie Dingle, the tall, long-armed redhead who replaced Marty, wasn't much more effective. The Catbirds scored three more runs before the Magpies could get them out.

Score: Catbirds 6, Magpies 4.

Artie led off with a walk in the bottom half of the third. Then Steve got a scratch hit, putting himself on first and Artie on second.

Dickie Stutz was walking toward the plate when Ted's voice boomed from the dugout: "Dickie, wait a minute!"

Ted came over and looked at Jamie. A grin spread across his even white teeth. "All right, Jamie. You're back in the game! Get up there and lay one down!"

Jamie's heart, rising in the knowledge he was back in the game, hit rock bottom again at Ted's last three words.

"What — again?" he exclaimed.

Ted laughed. "Again, Jamie. They'll expect you to hit away. Only, we can't take a chance of hitting into a double play. We've got to advance those runners. It's a surprise attack, Jamie. We need it — and you can do it."

"Oh — all right!" Jamie said despairingly. "You're the boss!"

He sprang from the bench, picked up his favorite bat and strode to the plate.

The pitch came in. His right hand slid down to the fat part of the bat.

A beautiful bunt!

The runners advanced one base. Jamie was thrown out at first, but that didn't matter.

Johnny Myers doubled and the ball game was tied up, 6-all.

Both teams continued to play heads-up ball. The game remained deadlocked until the top of the sixth, when Artie flied out and Steve grounded to short for the second out.

The crowd tensed. The Magpies' fans were shouting for a hit, the Catbirds' for a strikeout.

Once again it was Jamie's turn to bat. From behind he could hear his teammates urging him to send one out of the lot.

"Hit it!" he heard Ted Salin say. "Hit it, Jamie!"

He watched the first one breeze in. It was chest-high. He swung.

He connected solidly and started running around the bases. The tremendous roar that exploded from the grandstand told him it was a home run.

The Catbirds went down, one . . . two . . . three. The Magpies won, clinching the pennant.

Ted Salin shook Jamie's hand afterwards,

holding it in both of his. "I figured you'd pull out that plum sooner or later!" he grinned.

Jamie smiled warmly, sorry that he had ever thought Ted didn't know what he was doing.

"I guess sitting on the bench did me good!" he laughed.

U. S. 1930513

Stop That Puck!

TIM COURTNEY braced him-self in front of the net, his hockey stick gripped in both gloved hands. His eyes peered intently through the slot of his face guard. What a game! Nine to two in favor of the op-ponents, the Beavers. Good thing there were only a few minutes left in the game, or the Beavers would turn the game into the biggest slaughter the Bobcats had ever known.

The Beavers' speedy left forward, Monk Thomas, came skating toward the goal, drib-bling the puck. Tim waited breathlessly. Chip Flint, the Bobcats' strong left forward, glided in from Monk's left side and tried to steal the puck. Monk passed to another Beaver. Before

Tim could move, the puck sailed past his left skate into the net for another score.

"Come on, Tim!" Chip yelled. "You've got to move faster than that!"

Nobody had to tell Tim that. Of course he had to move faster. He just couldn't, that's all.

He glanced at the clock. One minute and twenty seconds to go, plenty of time for the Beavers to score another point or two. A poor attitude to take, but that's the way things were going. The Beavers were gnawing their way to a one-sided victory just because the Bobcats had a poor goalie.

The face-off. The referee dropped the puck between the two centers. Chip stole it from the Beaver center and dribbled it across the Bobcats' blue line. But a second later the ref blew his whistle. Fats Bailey, the Bobcats' chubby right guard, was off side.

A face-off in the Beavers' attacking zone. Chip and a Beaver forward struggled for the puck. Chip got it again. He smacked it across the center line. Nobody got it. It struck the boards and glanced behind the Beavers' goalie before a Beaver touched it.

The referee's whistle shrilled again. The official folded his arms, indicating the icing infraction, and the puck was brought back into the Bobcats' defensive zone for another face-off.

Left guard Jack Towns and a Beaver forward squared off for the puck. Their sticks clashed as they fought for control. Suddenly the puck skidded across the ice toward the net and Tim struck it with his stick, sending it against the boards at the right side.

"Thataway, Tim! Nice Save!" shouted the fans.

Oh, sure, he thought. Nice save, and we're trailing 10 to 2. Was somebody being funny?

The game finally ended, and he wished he could cut a hole in the ice and crawl into it. He skated to the locker room, hoping he wouldn't be seen in the crowd. Yet he heard someone yell, "Tough luck, Tim! Get em' the next time!"

Coach Jim Higgs had little to say. "The Beavers were on today and we were off," he said. "See you Tuesday night at practice. Are you going to make it, Tim?"

Tim had avoided his eyes. Now he looked up. The coach was eyeing him. "I'll try to," he said.

"You were at only one practice last week," reminded Coach Higgs. "If you want to play, you'll have to practice too, Tim. It's not fair to the other boys."

Tim's face colored. "I'll be there," he promised.

The game was the topic at the supper table. Mom, Dad, and Janie, Tim's younger sister, always attended the games and talked about them afterward. After a while the conversation changed to the skiing contest held on Berry Peak at the same time the Small Fry Hockey League played its games. Tim wished that he could have seen it.

"Cathy Erickson won it, I heard," said

Janie. "Next week she's competing in the finals."

"She ought to be good," said Tim. "She practically lives on those skis."

Janie's large brown eyes swung around to him. "Maybe if you'd practice more you'd be good too," she said.

The remark stung, and Tim made a face at her. "I was too busy to practice much last week, and anyway, why aren't you in the skiing contest, competing against Cathy?" he snapped back at her.

"I haven't skied as long as she has, that's why," replied Janie. "But next year I will. You wait and see."

"Okay, kids," said Mom, tapping a fork against the table top. "Better end it right here before things get any hotter."

"And melt both the ice and snow," added Dad. Janie and Tim laughed, then looked at each other.

"Well," Tim admitted, "Janie's right. I don't practice enough."

The phone rang. "I'll get it," said Janie. She

went to answer it and a moment later returned with a broad smile on her face. "It's Uncle Al!" she cried happily. "He and Aunt Marge are coming over this Saturday!"

"Good," smiled Mom. She looked beyond Janie toward the phone. "Janie, is Uncle Al still on the phone?"

"Oh, I forgot, he wants to talk to you, Daddy."

Tim looked at her and shook his head. What a crazy sister, he thought — forgetful, blunt and honest.

Suddenly Janie's words echoed and re-echoed in his mind. *"Uncle Al and Aunt Marge are coming over this Saturday."* His spirits dropped. Why did they have to come *this* Saturday?

Tim didn't need a second guess. They were coming because Uncle Al wanted to see the Bobcats play hockey, or rather, he wanted to see *Tim* play hockey. He had been a hockey star in college, had played professional hockey for a few years, and still played it to keep in shape. *One look at me as a goaltender and he'll be ashamed to claim me as a nephew,* Tim thought. *Why did I ever start playing hockey, anyway? Why wasn't I satisfied just to skate?*

When Tuesday rolled around Tim joined the practice session in the rink. The A Line played the B Line, with Tim playing for the A's. Butch Sales tended goal for the B's. After working out for half an hour, the lines rested. Butch, Tim noticed, was still at the net.

"Come on, some of you guys!" Butch yelled. "Try to drive that little black puck by me! Just try to!"

Chip grinned. "I think he wants to steal your job, Tim," he said.

"He can have it," replied Tim.

Chip stared at him. "What's the matter? I thought you liked playing goalie."

"I did. I don't anymore."

He still did, but he wasn't going to admit it to Chip. He kept looking at Butch. What did Butch think he was going to do, anyway?

Take over as first-string goalie? Talk about being slow — a snail could move faster than Butch!

The Bobcats practiced the next two nights. Butch and Tim were there both times. After a hard half-hour workout, Butch was still there in front of the net, challenging the guys to try to drive the puck past him. He was improving a lot, too. Tim watched him, a doubtful smile on his lips. Butch was too tall, too awkward. He'd never make a really good goalie.

Tim hated to see Saturday come. But it came, and so did Uncle Al and Aunt Marge.

"Had to see the Bobcats play before the season ended," said Uncle Al. "What's your team's record, Tim?"

"Won three, lost four," Tim answered soberly. "Nothing to brag about."

"Not bad. Win today and it'll be even up."

"Yeah," said Tim, not very enthusiastically.

He telephoned Butch Sales just before noon.

"Butch, I'm not feeling well. You want to tell Coach Higgs?"

"Got a cold, Tim?"

"I don't know what it is," said Tim.

"Okay. I'll tell the coach."

The game started at two o'clock. The seats around the rink were half-filled with hockey fans, mostly parents of the boys who played in the league. Tim was in uniform, but he was sitting on the bench. Butch Sales was playing goalie.

A minute and ten seconds after face-off, the Tigers, the Bobcats' opponents, punched in a goal. The puck had slid straight through Butch's legs.

I would have stopped that one, Tim told himself. Two minutes later, right after the B Line replaced the A Line on the ice, a Tiger socked in another goal.

Tim squirmed. That was another goal he was sure he could have prevented.

Chip scored a point. Then Butch managed to make a save that drew tremendous applause from the Bobcats' fans. Hardly half a minute later a Tiger charged in with the puck and zipped it like a bullet past Butch for their third goal.

Butch's head turned toward the Bobcats' bench, and even through the face guard Tim was able to see the worried look in Butch's eyes. Tim remembered what he had asked Butch to tell Coach Higgs. What an awful thing to do! What would Uncle Al and Aunt Marge think, if they knew that? They were sitting somewhere behind him, expecting to see him play. That was the only reason they had driven all the way from their home. Uncle Al had said so himself. But what had Tim done? He had pretended he didn't feel well so that Butch would play and take all the blame.

His throat ached. He got up and walked over to the coach. "Coach Higgs," he said, trembling a little. "Let me go in. Please."

Coach Higgs frowned. "I thought you didn't feel well. I was surprised that you even showed up."

"I — I just said that because my uncle is here today and I wasn't playing well," confessed Tim. "But, Butch — he just can't —"

Coach Higgs smiled. "Okay, Tim. Get ready."

A Tiger forward dribbled the puck across the center line and then across the Bobcats' blue line. Jack Towns tried to take it from him, but the Tiger passed it to another forward. The forward dribbled it toward the net, then snapped it.

Like a streak, the puck shot toward the left side of the net. Tim pounced on it like a cat and caught it in his mitt. A save!

"Yea!" screamed the fans. "Thataway to go, Tim!"

A few moments later, Chip blasted the puck past the Tigers' goalie. Bobcats, 2 — Tigers, 3. In the second period the Bobcats seemed to be back in form. They tied the score, then went into the lead 4 to 3, then 5 to 3. And Tim was making one save after

another. He missed one later, a high one that grazed past his ear, but the Tigers deserved that goal. The Bobcats scored again and the game ended 6 to 4 in the Bobcats' favor. And Tim had never been so happy — or so tired — in his life.

In the locker room, Coach Higgs and the guys praised him for his defensive job at the goal. "Guess practice paid off, didn't it, Tim?" Coach Higgs smiled. "And so did that extra effort."

"I guess it did," said Tim.

Then Uncle Al came in, a big smile on his face. "Say, fella, you really showed me something," he said. "I'm glad I came!"

Tim grinned as he took Uncle Al's outstretched hand. "So am I, Uncle Al," he said.

Baseballs and Bumblebees

YOU could tell it was spring. Baseballs were flying like happy, white butterflies fresh out of cocoons, and George Maxwell Jones was perched on a branch of a cherry tree, gently detaching handfuls of delectable fruit and eating them with gusto.

The tree, a mighty stanchion that had withstood many winter storms, was one of several on his father's land. Far below in the valley was the Jefferson High School baseball field, where figures were scooting around like worried ants.

George Maxwell Jones uttered a deepthroated sound in indignation at the sport going on down there and cast another hand-

ful of cherries into his mouth. Once or twice
he had pictured himself in a Jefferson High
uniform and had to admit to himself that it
didn't look bad on his six-foot-two frame.
Only when he visualized himself scampering
after a ground ball did he switch off the picture as he would a TV show. Somehow his
long legs never wanted to progress at any
speed that demanded extra exertion, and a
slowpoke could never make the team.

A bumblebee the size of a golf ball decided
just then to have some fun with George. He
made a semiorbit of the tree and charged in,
all afterburners turned on full. When George
saw the insect, he yelled and ducked. His
head hit a branch and bounded back like a
rubber ball. The bee came to a dead stop six
inches from George's nose. Suddenly it
zoomed and George moved with the most
exertion he had ever shown in his sixteen
years. He fell backward, and with a crashing
of branches and a scream, George went
through space. Trying to ease his fall, he put

out his hands. He made a one-point landing on a soft mound of earth and then felt pain in his right wrist that shot through his body like an electric charge. Once more George howled and then looked for the monster that had sent him to his disaster. The flying beast had landed on a glowing, bruised cherry and was, no doubt, sucking its delicious nectar.

"You rat!" said George.

He rose to his feet, brushed the dirt from his pants, and looked at his hurt wrist. There was a bump on its left side about the size of a large marble.

George had no way of knowing then that his fall was going to make him a figure of distinction at Jefferson High.

When his wrist continued to hurt the next day, he asked some of his friends what to do about it.

"Best way to cure a sore wrist is to throw a baseball," advised Eddie Vassy, second baseman for Jefferson High's baseball team. "Isn't that right, Walt?"

"And who knows better than me?" quipped the stocky, yellow-haired catcher who was having a pitch-and-catch game with Eddie. "Didn't I get a sore wrist last year? And didn't I throw to cure it?"

George looked uncertain. The boys were always kidding him, but these two seemed absolutely earnest about what they were saying now. Maybe this time they were being honest with him. Maybe Walt really did cure his sore wrist throwing a baseball.

"Here, try it," said Walt. He tossed the ball to George, who made an ungraceful stab at the ball and miraculously caught it. "Go ahead," Walt encouraged. "Throw it to Eddie. You remember; he's that boy standing there with the glove on his hand."

George gripped the clean white sphere between his thumb and first two fingers, reared back and threw. As the ball left his fingers pain pierced his wrist and he let out a violent yell. He cut the yell short, though, as he saw the ball suddenly twist into a spiral! Eddie's jaw dropped and his eyes widened in disbelief as he tried to follow the ball with his glove. It twisted in and hit him on the chest.

"Hey! Where'd you get that pitch?" cried Walt excitedly. "Never saw anything like that before in my life!"

"Don't throw it to me any more!" scowled Eddie, rubbing his sore chest. "Who do you think I am, Jerry Grote?"

"But, Eddie! That curve! Did you see how crazy it was?" Walt couldn't get over his amazement at George's throw. He was turning red with excitement and perspiring as if he had just completed a hundred-yard sprint. "Give me that ball, Eddie! I've got to see this hayseed do it again. You can do it again, can't you, George? Because if you can, you're the man our team's looking for. We didn't win a game last year, not one. Know why? We didn't have a pitcher, that's why. Not one guy could throw a single, measly curve. Here, George, throw him another one, just like that first one you threw."

"Not to me, he isn't!" yelled Eddie. "You come down here, pal! See how *you* like catching it on the chest!"

"Chicken!" said Walt, and ran down to replace Eddie. "Okay, George! Fire it!"

George stared intently at the baseball. A cold chill formed in a spot in his back and began to spread. He had thrown a baseball a few times in his life but it had never performed the way it had this time. Of course, it was an accident. He'd never do it again in a million years.

"Come on, George! Hurry up before the bell rings, will you?"

Scarcely had the words left Walt's lips when the bell began to shrill.

"George! Throw it, will you?"

Quickly, George reared back and once again fired the ball, aiming at the target Walt was giving him. Breathlessly he watched, wondering if the ball was going to repeat its fantastic performance. It was shooting straight as a bullet toward the outside of Walt's glove. Then, suddenly, it cut sharply to the left, curved up, shot to the right exactly as it did before! Walt was a little better in getting a glove on it than Eddie. The ball struck his thumb and *then* his chest.

"You did it again, George!" screamed Walt.

"What kind of a pitch is it?" asked Eddie excitedly. "What do you call it, George?"

George's brows rose as far as they could go. "Kind of pitch?" he asked. "How should I know?" And then he turned and ran toward the open door of the school. "Come on! The bell's rung!" he cried over his shoulder.

At practice that afternoon it didn't take Coach Bobo Wilson more than ten seconds to recognize outstanding performance when he saw it. He was even satisfied by the brief rejoinder, "I don't know," to his question: "Where and how did you learn to throw that crazy curve?" The coach even had to teach George how to stand on the rubber when the neophyte pitcher prepared to make his delivery. George had never played baseball in his life and didn't know any of the rules.

"Just throw that ball over the plate and don't balk," said Coach Wilson. "Those are the only rules you have to worry about, kid! Keep pitching like that and you'll break our losing streak!"

Barton High was Jefferson's first opponent. The game was on a Tuesday, right after school, and a crowd had assembled even before the teams got onto the field. Evidently word of George Maxwell Jones and his crazy curve ball had spread like wildfire. The sky was overcast, the air warm, and George's wrist, although the bump had not changed in shape or size, felt fine.

The teams had their pregame warm-up, and Jefferson took the field. The coach had procured the biggest mitt he could find for Walt to catch George's throws. George lobbed three pitches with just enough thrust to get them to the catcher. Then Walt pegged to second and the umpire shouted: "Play ball!"

George waited for the batter to step into the box. He was prickling with excitement as he got in position on the mound exactly as Coach Wilson had instructed him. He stood tall as a giant, a proud glimmer in his eyes. He remembered dreaming about this.

Without winding up George reared back, lifted his left leg high, brought his arm around and released the ball with only part of his strength. It was silly to throw any harder than he had to, yet.

The ball shot straight for the plate. Unless it switched plans it would be a perfect strike, or be lambasted for a long hit. Then, about two-thirds of the way, it shot into its crazy pattern. The batter, who had prepared to swing at a beautiful straight ball, stared.

"Strike!" said the umpire as the ball corkscrewed over the plate.

The ball struck the edge of Walt's mitt and dropped to the ground. Walt picked it up hastily and tossed it back to George.

"Thataway, George, ol' boy! Beautiful pitch! Beautiful!"

George rubbed the ball with satisfaction, stepped on the mound and threw again. This time the ball favored the outside corner. Was it actually too far out? It was hard to tell, but it made no difference. The batter swung at it for strike two.

"Time!" yelled the batter, holding up an angry hand at the umpire. "Take a look at the ball, ump! No baseball can do what that one's doing!"

Walt laughed. "Sure! Here, look at it!"

The umpire took the ball from Walt, curled it around in his hand, and said, "If it's a trick ball, I can't see it. Anyway, here's another one."

He took a brand new baseball out of his pocket, handed it to Walt, and stuffed the other ball back into his pocket.

"Play ball!" he ordered.

Walt tossed the ball to George. George caught it and stepped into the pitcher's box. He waited till the batter got ready, then reared back and aimed the throw for Walt's huge mitt.

The ball left his hand quite naturally, sped in a straight line, then went into its spiral. The batter gawked. His jaw sagged open and he made a futile and late attempt at a swing.

"You're out!" bellowed the umpire.

One hundred and sixty fans cheered and whistled. The second batter was no better than the first, nor the third better than the second. Inning after inning, George Maxwell Jones threw the ball the only way he knew how and let it take its unnatural course.

This is how the game continued until twenty-seven Barton High men were out. George had walked four, thrown four wild pitches, and six batters had managed to tick the ball for a foul. But Barton High didn't score, and Jefferson won the game, 3 to 0, breaking its streak of eleven losses.

George was hoisted on stocky shoulders and carried like a hero to the school locker room. Everyone began shaking his hand — his left one — so that his right would be well enough to go again in the next game. Coach Wilson actually had a teary glimmer in his eyes as he praised his newly-discovered hurler.

Davidson High was the next to falter under

George's unorthodox curve. Three times as many spectators as before witnessed the game. There was even a photographer who took pictures of George in various positions on the mound. George, unaccustomed to such accolades, blushed most of the time.

"What do you call that pitch?" a reporter asked as he cornered George before the hero could get off the playing field.

"Don't call it anything," replied George innocently.

"You don't have a name for it?"

"No," said George. "No name. I just throw it, that's all."

"Did anybody teach it to you? A big leaguer? Or a friend who knows how to pitch?"

"No," repeated George. "I just throw it, that's all."

"Amazing!" murmured the reporter. "Kid, some big league team will snatch you up quicker than you can say George — by the way, what's your full name?"

"George Maxwell Jones."

"That's a mouthful, isn't it?"

"Sure is," said George.

Washington High fell next, and then Clemson and St. James went down before George's corkscrew pitch. On two occasions Steve Buckner had to relieve George on the mound. Both times George was hit by a pitched ball — once on his foot, and once on his left elbow. In each case the incidents happened during the last two innings when Jefferson was ahead. Coach Wilson wanted to protect his star hurler from possible serious injuries, so he pulled him. An ordinary baseball player could have dodged the pitches easily, but, of course, George Maxwell Jones was no ordinary baseball player.

Big league scouts came to witness his fantastic performance, and there wasn't one who wouldn't have signed him on the spot — if it had been legal to sign up high school players. George could hardly wait till he graduated. Walt had told him that some bonus babies signed for a hundred thousand dollars! Just imagine that! A hundred thousand dollars!

The season ended with Jefferson High copping the pennant and the championship. George Maxwell Jones was named the most valuable player of the year. If that wasn't enough, he was also selected as an all-state player.

During summer vacation George liked to relax on his father's farm. The apple trees there provided plenty of good places to sit and dream of a big league future.

George was sitting in one of these trees, picking off the small green but delicious apples, when a large bumblebee, yellow, with black stripes on its back approached.

It droned along sleepily, but suddenly it picked up speed and dodged around a score of apples as if it were a contestant in a race. George watched it; a nerve began to tingle at the base of his back. The bee banked sharply to the left, and headed directly for George's head.

"No!" shouted George, and reared backward hastily.

There was nothing at his back to catch him and he plunged to the ground. He put out his hands to cushion his fall and made a three-point landing. He groaned as pain shot through his tall, lean frame. George sat there momentarily, watching the bumblebee buzzing around the apples. In a little while, as if not satsified with what it found, the bee streaked away, a bolt of yellow, at a speed that looked as if it could well break the sonic barrier.

George snarled as he rose to his feet. He brushed off his pants and felt his right wrist. He had removed the tape from his pitching arm after the season had ended, and now he looked at it with a dismal sensation coming over him. He turned his wrist this way and that and felt no pain at all.

He stared at it with foreboding. He hurried home, got his glove, and called on Walt.

"What gives, man?" said Walt, staring. "The season's been over a long time."

"I want to throw one pitch," George told Walt, breathlessly. "Just one is all I'll need."

Walt looked at him as if George had cracked up, but without further argument he got his mitt and took his stance about sixty feet away from George. He only had his regular-size mitt at home during the summer, and a worried frown marked his face.

George looked at the target Walt gave him, reared back, and threw. The ball streaked straight as an arrow — all the way to Walt's mitt. It didn't curve up, down, or sideways. It didn't spiral. It didn't do anything. It just went straight.

"Just what I thought," murmured George sadly. "It's all over, Walt."

"It didn't curve!" yelled Walt, horrified. "It's the first one that didn't curve!"

"I know," said George, looking at his wrist.

"Throw me another!" cried Walt. "You can't lose that curve just like that!"

"But I have," murmured George. "It's gone!"

He proved it when he threw again — a perfect straight ball so wide of Walt's target Walt almost missed catching it.

So ended George Maxwell Jones' pitching days.

But to this day his name is remembered and is inscribed on a tall, golden trophy displayed in the hall of Jefferson High:

"In honor of our hero, George Maxwell Jones, pitcher of eleven straight victories for Jefferson High School."

To this day George can never see a bee without smiling slightly and shaking his head. Some of his friends know his story, but others wonder why he acts that way.

No Spot for Jerry

JERRY BELL braced himself and looked directly into the blue eyes of the guard opposite him.

"One! Two! Hip!" Quarterback Dave Wheeler's voice snapped like a whip.

At the cry, "Hip!" the lines lunged at each other. Jerry pushed forward and felt himself thrust aside. The next instant he was sprawled on the ground, his brown and white helmet cocked slightly on his head.

All around him was a tangle of brown and green uniforms. The pileup was behind him. He got to his feet as quickly as he could.

The referee's whistle pierced the air, and the pile unscrambled. At the bottom was Mike

Towns, fullback for the Browns. His helmet was pushed over his eyes. Dirt smeared his cheeks.

"Huddle," snapped Dave Wheeler.

In the huddle Mike looked dagger-eyed at Jerry. "That guard busted right through you," he said. "That's the second time. Can't you stop him?"

Jerry blushed. "I tried," he said timidly.

"Okay," said Dave. "We'd better try a pass. Twelve flair."

Twelve flair meant the pass would be either to right end Fred Jones or left end Bert Buck.

The huddle broke. The teams lined up with the Browns in T formation. The Indians formed a five, four, two defense. The ball was on the Browns' thirty-eight-yard line. It was third down and thirteen to go.

"Twelve! Nine! Green!" barked Dave.

The center snapped the ball. Dave took it and handed it to right halfback Jim Philips. Jim faded back, yanked the ball to his shoulder and heaved it. The ball shot across the field but wobbled and fell short almost in the hands of an Indians player.

"Pass incomplete," yelled the referee.

"We have to kick," said Dave in the huddle. "Okay, Mike. It's up to you."

Mike caught the snap from center and booted it hard down the field. The pigskin soared high for twenty-five yards. An Indians player caught it and carried it back to their forty-one.

The Indians moved down the field steadily, picking up first downs as if there were nothing to it. Jerry felt helpless. He was the tallest on the team and the most awkward. This was the Browns' first game of the season and Jerry's second year as a football player — if you could call him that.

Coach Ward had tried Jerry at tackle, guard, and end during practice sessions. Jerry didn't seem to click at any position. His feet did not lift when he wanted them to, nor did his body move the way he wanted it to go. There was no use trying him in a backfield spot. You had to be fast to play in one of those positions.

The Browns stopped the Indians for a while. Then before the first quarter was over, the Indians scored a touchdown. They kicked the extra point to give them a 7 to 0 lead.

Coach Ward put in substitutes during the second quarter. Jerry warmed the bench, wondering whether he would go back in again.

With four minutes to go, the coach put Jerry in at right tackle. Jerry's man was too quick for him. He slipped past Jerry like an eel whenever the Browns had the ball. He blocked Jerry like a brick wall when the Indians had possession.

I'm just a scrub, thought Jerry. I'm no good here at all. But I can't quit; I love to play football.

On the Browns' twelve-yard line, the Indians tried a pass. The throw was too high. Defensive right halfback Jim Philips intercepted it and raced all the way down the field for a touchdown. Mike kicked the extra point, and the score was tied 7 to 7.

The cheerleaders sprang in front of the fans and gave three cheers for Jim. Seconds later the half ended.

In the locker room Coach Ward talked to his boys a bit, pointing out their errors and their good plays. Then the team went out on the field to pass a couple of footballs among themselves.

Jerry mingled with the others. He got the ball often and heaved it far out to whomever called for it. His throws were like bullets and accurate almost every time. He enjoyed this. At least he could throw a football and throw it well.

The Indians showed their strength again at the start of the third quarter. Within two minutes they scored a touchdown. Their try for the extra point missed, and the score was Indians 13, Browns 7.

Late in the quarter, the Indians threatened to score again, but the Browns held them.

In the fourth, quarterback Dave Wheeler tried almost every play the Browns knew to gain yardage. Yet, at the end of each series of downs, they would always have to punt to put the ball as far away as possible from their goal line.

Jerry was on the bench. Suddenly, Coach Ward looked at him.

"Jerry, go out in Jim Philips' place. Tell Dave to call the twelve flair play. I saw you throw that ball during the half. Let me see you throw it the same way in the game."

Jerry's eyes widened. His mouth became dry.

"I'll try, Coach."

Jerry ran in. Dave and all the players stared unbelievingly at him as he repeated what the coach had said.

The ball was on the Browns' twenty-three-yard line. It was first and ten.

"Twelve! Two! Blue!"

The ball snapped from center. Dave faked to Mike, then stepped back and handed the ball to Jerry. Jerry took it, faded back, and looked at the two men, Fred Jones and Bert Buck, who were running out for the pass.

Bert was farthest away and in the clear. Jerry heaved the ball to him. It sailed high and long. Then it came down right into Bert's arms. He pulled it to him and raced on down the field for a touchdown.

The Browns' fans sprang to their feet and yelled lustily. What a beautiful throw! What a magnificent catch!

Mike kicked the pigskin between the up-rights for the extra point, putting the Browns ahead, 14 to 13.

The Indians couldn't do much after that. Their spirit seemed broken by the Browns' unexpected score. Soon the game was over. Dave, Mike — they all pounded Jerry on the back and shook his hand.

Coach Ward came over, his face covered with a big grin. "I know where there's a spot for you now," he told Jerry happily.

Substitute Sophomore

THE sharp crack of the baseball as it struck the deep pocket of the catcher's mitt echoed off the barn door and resounded in the rolling meadow beyond. Feeling the sting against his swollen palm, Durwin Ackroyd raised himself again to his stocky, five-foot-eight height and looped the ball back to his older, taller brother.

Perc's sunbronzed face broke into a soft smile. "Holler if I'm throwing 'em too hard, kid," he said.

Durwin smiled halfheartedly as he tugged at his pantlegs and crouched back into position. "Maybe you've got a smoke arm," he said, "but you've got to do a lot better than that to pulverize this guy's hand!"

He raised the mitt up to his right side as a target for Perc, then watched as Perc lifted up his arms, brought them down and fired the ball toward him. Perc was over six feet, thin as a guard rail, so that when he stretched to release the ball it seemed he was a third of the way to the piece of board that represented home plate. The ball came in as if it had been shot from a Winchester rifle. It cut in a sharp hook right for the spot where Durwin had made a target. Durwin made a lightning move to snare the bullet-like ball, and the resounding smack of horsehide against the mitt sang out again over the fields and meadow.

After a few more throws Perc wiped the sweat from his sunbleached brows and called it enough. Durwin pulled the glove off his hand and looked at the swollen flesh. Perc came over and took a look.

"Well!" he exclaimed good-humoredly. "Not pulverized, huh? What do you want it to look like? Hamburger?"

His hand throbbed, but Durwin didn't

mind. "You should've seen it yesterday," he grinned.

The next day was Monday, which meant baseball practice after school. Perc pitched a little for batting practice, and the coach had Rusty Woods catch him. Chuck Wesley relieved Rusty, and finally Durwin took a turn catching. Batting practice was a routine and monotonous chore for Durwin. He was a sophomore, and he felt that he was hardly present as far as the coach was concerned. He was sure that if he failed to show up for practice tomorrow afternoon the coach would never miss him.

That night in bed Durwin had plenty of time to think the whole thing over. He considered playing one of the infield positions, but visualizing his small stature trying to nab a high throw from short was comical. He rolled over in bed and tried to picture himself dashing after a hot grounder near the keystone bag. He saw his stubby legs churning the air but his stocky form getting no place.

Perhaps there was a place for him in the outfield. He might be able to perform a little better out there, but probably not well enough. No, he couldn't see where he could fit in except as a catcher. And he couldn't make even that, he thought bitterly.

Durwin didn't show up for practice the next night. When Perc came home, he looked with puzzlement at his sophomore brother.

"Where were you?" he asked. "Why didn't you show up?"

Durwin shrugged. "The coach say anything?"

"No. But if you do that again he might take you off the team. You know that, don't you?"

"Yeah. I know that," he said. But, he thought grimly, how would the coach know if he didn't even miss him? "I just catch 'em before the game starts," he said. "A warmerupper, that's me."

Perc didn't answer. He looked away, turned, and walked casually toward the house.

* * *

In the game Thursday against Berkshire, Perc performed like a veteran for St. Lucy's. For three innings he set them down without a hit. St. Lucy's meanwhile picked up a run in the second. In the fourth, Berkshire's first baseman slugged a line drive over short for a neat single. A sacrifice bunt put him on second, and an error by the shortstop, Cal Miller, gave him third. Perc struck out the next batter, but his first pitch to the following man proved costly. It was his fast hook, dropping sharply across the outside corner of the plate, and Rusty couldn't get his mitt there quick enough. The ball whizzed through him and bounded back to the bleachers.

The runner sped home to tie the score, 1 to 1. Durwin saw the coach kick his spiked heel into the dirt, and chew harder on his gum.

The next man up lined a double to right field and then second baseman Tommy Meirs booted one that gave the opponents another run to put them in the lead 2 to 1. Perc fanned the next batter.

In the sixth, St. Lucy's tied the score on a three-bagger that brought in a man from first. A wild peg over first by Berkshire's shortstop scored another run. St. Lucy's continued in the lead up to the eighth when Berkshire's pitcher, who had fanned twice so far, got onto one for three bases.

"Lucky stiff!" grunted Durwin.

The lead-off man came up and swung at the first pitch. He ticked it for a foul; the ball took a vicious hop into the catcher's waiting mitt. Suddenly the ball was on the ground in front of Rusty, and Rusty was flinging off his mitt and hugging his hand.

"Time!" yelled the umpire.

The coach leaped forward, followed by Chuck and Durwin. From the box Perc was running in, too.

"What happened, Rusty?" the coach said.

The boy seemed to be too much in pain to speak. He lifted his right hand and showed two swollen, bruised fingers.

"Okay, kid," the coach said. "You'll need

first aid right away. Chuck — Durwin, help him take off his stuff."

As Durwin proceeded to remove Rusty's shin guards, he heard the coach say to Perc, "Boy! If that isn't tough luck!"

"Sure is," agreed Perc.

The coach drew in a deep breath and expelled it. He scratched the back of his neck and looked around at Durwin and Chuck. A hopeless expression seemed to settle in his grey eyes.

Finally he said, "Okay, Chuck. Get in there in place of Rusty."

Durwin glanced at Chuck, saw the boy's face cloud with worry. He knew what had passed suddenly through Chuck's mind.

Durwin looked at Perc and met his brother's eyes. His heart started pounding. He stepped up to the coach.

"Coach, let me get in. I can catch Perc. We've . . . practiced."

The coach gazed soberly at him.

"Honest! I can do it!" Durwin pleaded.

The coach turned to Perc. "What do you think, Perc?"

Perc grinned. "I think he'll surprise you, Coach," he said.

The coach smiled, tapped Durwin's shoulder. "Okay, kid. Get on those guards. Surprise me."

After a few warmup pitches, the umpire called time in and Durwin, his heart thumping wildly, crouched behind the batter and signaled Perc for a curve. The lead-off man was still up. He cut at the ball and missed. Durwin whipped the mitt over fast and snared the pill.

"Strike tuh!" cried the umpire.

"Come on, Perc!" Durwin yelled, settling down into the game now. "Let's get 'im outa there!"

Perc reeled in a fast drop. Again the batter swung.

"Strike threeeee!" said the umpire.

Durwin grinned. He caught Perc's glance. Perc winked and he winked back. They were in this together.

The next hitter popped a fly to short for out number two. One more to go, thought Durwin. The tying run was on third, the possible winning run was at the plate. They just had to get this man out.

Durwin signaled for one low inside. Perc nodded, lifted his arms and delivered. The ball shot toward the plate almost exactly to the spot where Durwin held his glove. The batter swung.

There was a crack; the ball bounded across the diamond between short and third. Cal Miller darted for it. Coming home was the runner from third, running as fast as he could in an effort to tie the score.

Miller snared the ball, heaved it in. The crowd's roar was in his ears as Durwin straddled home plate and waited for the long throw. It looked as if it might be a tie. Then the ball was there slamming into his mitt. He fell with it in front of the plate. He felt spikes graze his glove as a shower of dust blasted into his face.

He didn't know what the call would be.

It was that close. Then he rose, and hands began to pound his back. Voices cheered in his ears. He saw Perc's grinning face, and he knew the inning was over.

They scored no runs in the ninth, but neither did Berkshire. The game was over.

In the dressing room Perc said, "What did I tell you, Coach?"

The coach smiled happily. "I wasn't sure about him after he missed practice yesterday, and I was kind of worried about next year since you're graduating," he said. Then he grinned at Durwin. "But since I've still got one Ackroyd left on my club, I'm not worried anymore!"

Full Throttle

"YOU going in?"

"Why not?" Chick Grover eyed his friend Butch Slade as if he were surprised Butch could even think of such a question. "Maybe Mort's forgotten."

"Mort never forgets," replied Butch, turning to look through the large plate glass window of *Mort's Pit Stop*. "He's like an elephant."

"Yeah, I know," said Chick. "In more ways than one. Anyway, I'll try. Maybe he won't see me in that crowd."

He saw the usual Saturday afternoon slot car fans huddled in front of the track. Racers were zooming down the straightaways, blast-

ing around the S-curve and sweeper at speeds
so fast his eyes swam trying to keep up with
them.

Chick recognized Jack Harmon. It was
Jack's fault that Chick had been booted out of
Mort's Pit Stop last Friday evening during the
Semi-Main event. Chick's Lotus Formula 1
was on its twenty-seventh lap, two behind
Jack's Lola T-70, when Jack met his bomb on
the S-curve and nerfed the Lotus clear off
the track. It had landed on the floor with a
crash that destroyed the motor and part of
the chassis, and chipped a piece off the hand-
some, sleek, ocean-green body.

Chick knew as sure as anything that Jack
Harmon had done it on purpose, even though
Jack said he hadn't. He had lit into Jack with
fists flying, knocking him against a corner of
the slot car race track hard enough to jar the
track and deslot half of the cars racing.

So what did that elephant-sized Mort Yates
do? Blamed the whole shebang on Chick,
that's what. Told him to get out and stay out.

If that wasn't the unfairest deal a guy could pull, Chick didn't know what was.

"Well, you coming or aren't you?"

Chick saw that Butch had already opened the door. "I told you I was, didn't I?"

He realized his grumpiness and apologized. "Sorry, Butch."

He used to think that he got some satisfaction from being grumpy, that it gave him a feeling of being better than the next guy. Then there were times when grumpiness made him feel lousy. Just as lousy as one can get. And that was when he became ashamed of himself.

"I'll hide in the crowd while you get your controller," Chick suggested.

Butch headed for the counter where Mort Yates was adjusting a motor on a slot car for a kid.

Six of the eight lanes were taken. The two not taken were on the outside. The two un-occupied drivers' seats were at the far right. Chick pressed up behind the last one and settled down to watch the race.

Jack Harmon's blue Lola T-70 carried a yellow dot and was on Lane 7, the yellow lane, second from the inside. It was a classy bomb. Jack had won more ribbons and trophies with it than any other slot car driver in Chesterton.

Chick was secretly jealous of Jack because of it. He sometimes thought that he disliked Jack because he was better than anyone else in almost everything he did. And Jack picked on him a lot, too.

Ken Jason was there, using his own pistol-grip controller. His car was a Ford GTP, a two-toned, black and yellow model that had twice won the Concours d'Elégance, an event for the best-looking car model. It was racing on the blue Number 4 lane.

Ken and Jack, sitting side by side, had their eyes glued to their cars. Turn marshals were stationed at the four sharp curves.

Butch Slade shouldered through the crowd, sat beside Ken, and plugged in his controller. A green dot was on the hood of his black Porsche. He opened his oil of wintergreen pad, ran the rear wheels back and forth across it to goop up the tires, then placed the car on the green Number 2 lane.

Ken shot a quick glance at Butch. "Hi, Butch."

"Hi, Ken."

Jack Harmon looked over at Butch and spoke, too. Then he looked at Chick and surprise replaced the calm expression on his face.

"Chick!" You could've heard him in the next county. "Thought you weren't supposed to come in here anymore."

"Why don't you fall into a volcano?" snapped Chick sourly.

The Lola was on the upper level of the track. Jack whizzed it around the sweeper, the steep, wide bank at the right side of the track, stopped it in front of himself, picked it up, fiddled with the brushes a second, then rose from his chair and headed for the counter. *Oh-oh*, thought Chick. *That sneak. Pretending something's wrong with his car when all*

*he wants to do is squeal on me. And what am
I doing? Nothing but watching.*

Seconds later Jack returned and continued
racing his Lola. Mort didn't come. Maybe
Jack hadn't squealed, after all. Maybe he was
as honest as he always pretended to be.

Then a hand rested on Chick's shoulder. A
strong, heavy hand. Chick looked around and
there stood Mort Yates, all six-foot-one of
him, staring down as if he had caught Chick
robbing the First National Bank.

"Out, Chick."

"Why? What did I do? I haven't done anything."

"I want to make sure you don't," said Mort
curtly. "Come on."

The people opened up a hole and Chick
ambled through, ashamed and hurt. Mort
opened the door and Chick walked out, hands
stuck stiffly into his pockets.

I haven't done a thing! he thought bitterly.
Not a thing!

"Hey, Chick!" yelled Butch Slade. "Wait for me! I'll be out as soon as I finish!"

Chick trembled and got as close to crying as he had in a long time. He suddenly felt empty and alone.

Louse! That's what Mort Yates was. A big, dumb louse who just loved to show how tough he was.

After a while Jack Harmon and Ken Jason came out of the building, carrying metal boxes which held their slot cars and accessories.

"You squealer!" snarled Chick. "You snitched on me!"

Jack's mouth curved. "I did not snitch," he said.

"Liar!" Chick sailed into him, fists doubled up. Just as he was about to land a blow Jack lifted his metal box. It stopped Chick's blow and sent a sharp pain up his arm that jarred him all the way down to his heels.

"I told you I didn't snitch on you!" shouted Jack angrily. "You're making it up!"

"Coward!" yelled Chick, rubbing his aching bruised fist.

"Hey, you kids! Stop that fighting!" a loud, authoritative voice rang out from up the street.

Heavy feet pounded on the sidewalk and a moment later Police Officer Tom Duffy was beside them. "All right now, Chick. Just control yourself and tell me what it's all about."

Chick. It was always *Chick.*

2

Chick explained to Officer Duffy what it was all about. Jack didn't speak up until Chick had finished his explanation.

"That isn't so, Mr. Duffy. I didn't nerf his car on purpose. Ken can tell you that, too."

"Keep me out of it," said Ken.

"Okay, okay," said Tom Duffy. "You two guys go on your way. I want to talk with Chick alone."

Jack and Ken left and Tom Duffy looked at Chick. "Chick, whether you're right or not —"

"But I *am* right!"

"Look, I've known Jack since he was a little boy, Chick. I've never known him to tell a lie that would get a person in trouble."

"But this time was diff —"

"Now, just a minute. Let me finish. Just suppose Jack did do on purpose what you said he's done. Did you have to fly into him after what happened to you last Friday night? You're just piling up demerits till you'll have a reputation that'll stretch from here to San Francisco. And you won't have to wonder what friends you'll have either. You won't have any. You'll be as lonesome as a polecat." Tom Duffy paused and smiled. "And that's really lonesome. You want to be like that?"

Chick tried to keep from smiling back, but he couldn't. "No, I guess not, Mr. Duffy," he said quietly.

"Well, then?"

Chick shrugged. "I'll try not to pop off the next time."

Tom Duffy laughed and ruffled Chick's

hair. "That a boy, Chick. By the way, how are your daddy and mom?"

"Oh, fine, I guess."

The door of *Mort's Pit Stop* opened and Butch Slade came out. "Hi, Mr. Duffy," he greeted.

"Hi, Butch. How'd you do?"

"Came in third in a Wildcat race. Of course, there were only four of us racing."

Tom Duffy chuckled, said goodbye with a salute and a final remember-what-I-said look at Chick, and walked away.

"What did he have to say?" asked Butch.

"Plenty," replied Chick.

They walked along silently for a while, Chick trying to scratch Tom Duffy's words out of his mind but with no success. No matter what Tom Duffy or anybody said, Jack Harmon was to blame for all the trouble he'd been getting into. And fistfighting with Jack wasn't settling matters one bit. It just made them worse.

There was only one place their feud could

be settled, and that was on a slot car racing track.

But how could he race without a car?

"I'd like to build a car, but where could I race it, Butch? Think Ken will let me race it on his track?"

"Ask him," said Butch.

They walked to Ken's house and Chick knocked on the door. "Ken here, Mrs. Jason?" he asked as Ken's mother opened the door.

"Hello, Chick. Yes, just a second. Ken! Someone to see you!"

In a moment Ken appeared.

"Hi, guys."

"Hi. Ken, if I build a scratch kit racer would you let me run it on your track? Mort won't let me set foot in his place any more."

"I don't know," said Ken. "I'll have to ask my father."

Chick stared at him. "What?"

"Well, it belongs to both of us."

"Oh — well, forget it, Ken. Maybe I can't buy a scratch kit, anyway."

"If you do, then come back, Chick. I'm sure my dad won't mind. Really."

"Okay. Thanks, Ken. See ya."

A father owning a model car racing track with his son was all right, Chick supposed. But did the son *have* to ask him if it were all right for some other kid to race a car on it?

Well — if you invited a kid who didn't care. A kid who messed around and popped off at other people. In that case, yes. You had to go along with his father then.

That evening, after supper, Chick mustered all the nerve he could and asked his father for six dollars and forty-nine cents, the cost of a cheap slot car kit at *Mort's Pit Stop* (providing Mort would let him buy it — and why shouldn't he?).

Dad's answer was no surprise.

"Can't right now, Chick. It's the end of the month. Bill paying time."

Just what Chick had thought. It was the same every time, whether it was at the end of the month, the middle, or the beginning. He just had no chance.

He picked up Whitey, the fluffy white cat, put him on his lap and stroked him. One thing about cats: they never had problems.

3

At school Monday, Chick Grover got the surprise of his life. He had told Butch his dad wasn't able to give him any money to purchase a slot car kit, and the word got around to Jack Harmon.

"I have a car you can buy for two-fifty," offered Jack. "I've had it for a long time, but it's a good one. It's worth all of that price."

"I haven't got two-fifty. I haven't got a dime."

"You can pay me when you get it," said Jack.

Chick stared at him. "What kind of car is it?"

"A Ferrari. The paint's chipped off some and she's banged up a little, but that won't stop her from running. It's old, so you have to be careful with it, that's all."

"I'll take it," said Chick, "when I get the money."

Chick had a speed test in math and flunked it. Math bugged him. Mom and Dad used to help him with it, but neither one could make heads or tails out of it now. Mr. Cullen, the math teacher, said it was easy as falling off a log and Chick would realize that if he'd concentrate instead of spending most of his time drawing pictures of racing cars.

After school Chick asked the neighbors if he could cut their lawns, pick their weeds, carry out their garbage, anything. But no one had a thing for him to do. Their husbands or sons did those jobs.

Dad was his only answer. That night Chick talked to him again. "Dad, I could buy a slot car for two-fifty. Jack Harmon will sell it to me. I've looked all over for a job to raise the money but I can't find one. I'll do anything you want me to, Dad, honest, if you'll —"

"Well, well, well!" exclaimed Dad, and looked at his wife. "Mary, did you hear what I heard, or are my ears deceiving me?"

"They're not deceiving you," she said. "I heard every word."

He turned back to Chick. "Okay, son. I'll let you have two-fifty on condition you get down to brass tacks on your math and bring home a better-looking report card. I know you can do better. You're not a dumbbell. Especially in math. Who did you say you're buying the car from?"

"Jack Harmon."

"Isn't he the kid you're always scrapping with?"

Chick shrugged. "Yes. But if I don't buy the car from him I won't have one. I — I guess you don't really understand how much I miss having one. Only a kid would understand that."

His father took two one-dollar bills and a

fifty-cent piece out of his wallet, placed it in front of Chick, then took Chick's hand.

"I was a young boy, too, son. I remember once I wanted something very bad. A bike. A two-wheeler. A crummy-looking two-wheeler that needed a paint job, a new tire, and repair work on the chain. The kid was asking five dollars for it. I didn't have that kind of money. My father was dead. My mother was the only one working, trying to raise five kids. That was why I . . . I — " He cleared his throat and looked away for a moment. "Anyway, I didn't get the five dollars. I didn't get the bike. I never had a bike in my life, Chick."

The next day Chick gave Jack Harmon the two-fifty for the old, beat-up Farrari, then asked Ken Jason again if he could race on his track.

"Sure, you can, Chick."

"Aren't you going to ask your father?"

"I asked him the first time you asked me." Ken laughed. "He said it was okay."

"Oh." Chick smiled. "Okay. I'll come over."

Butch Slade was there when Chick arrived at Ken's after supper on Wednesday. The track was in the basement. It was the sharpest home track Chick had ever seen. It was triple-laned and laid out on a four by eight-foot plyboard. There were two long straightaways, overhead ramps, a sharp S-curve at one end and a U-curve at the other.

There were also trees, a grandstand and a pit stop where three 1/24-inch scale model cars were being "handled" by track "mechanics." For a long time Chick just stood, thrilled by the sight that looked so real. *I'd give anything for a track like this*, he thought. *Anything.*

But he knew he'd never have a track like this. Never. Not while he was still a kid.

"Go ahead," said Ken. "Try out your new bomb."

"*New* bomb?" Chick laughed. "It's older'n a monkey's uncle."

He placed the Ferrari on the track, picked up the controller, and Ken turned on the power. The controller was the kind you pushed down with your thumb. The farther down you pushed it, the more power went to the motor, and faster went the car.

Chick thumbed the controller. The Ferrari jerked ahead, roared up the far left ramp and spun out on the sharp curve.

Butch put the flag back into the slot, straightened the car and Chick thumbed the controller again. The car crawled around the S-curve and Chick full-throttled it down the opposite straightaway. Too late he realized the car was speeding too fast. It left the track, spun over the white fence and crashed to the hard, cement floor.

"Track!" yelled Butch, laughing.

Chick stared at the Ferrari. It was a shambles. Its front axle, with wheels intact, had come off the frame and was rolling toward the far wall. The flag was broken off.

But the worst sight of all was the motor. It

was hanging outside of the overturned car, its
two wires, a green and a red, still clinging to
the broken flag.

"That lousy Jack Harmon!" cried Chick,
choking back tears. "He lied to me! He lied
to me again!"

4

Chick Grover lit into Jack Harmon the
following day in the corridor of the school.

"You sold me a lemon!" he shouted, his
voice carrying through the full length of the
corridor. "A lousy piece of junk!"

Jack stuck by his guns. "I told you that the
car was old and you had to be careful with it,"
he said. "It's not my fault your head's as fat as
a balloon."

Chick's ears turned as red as a stoplight.
"You know what I'm going to do? I'm going
to build a car and beat the pants off you! I'm
going to beat you so bad you'll wish you took

up tiddlywinks, Mr. Jack Wise-Guy Harmon!"

"Well, well, well! What's this all about?" a dry, husky voice broke in.

Mr. Webber, the principal, was coming up the hall, his heels clicking on the tiled floor. He was only four inches taller than Chick, but he had the shoulders, chest and neck of the college football guard he had been once upon a time.

"What's this about beating someone's pants off?" he said, stepping between Chick and Jack and looking from one boy to the other.

"Nothing," said Chick, and started to walk away.

Mr. Webber grabbed his arm. "I've asked a question, Chick. What's this about beating someone's pants off?"

"I sold him a slot car and it got damaged when he raced it last night," explained Jack. "He blames me for it."

"Who wouldn't?" snapped Chick. "It was a piece of junk."

"You still didn't answer my question,' snapped Mr. Webber.

"I told him I'm going to build a car and beat his pants off," said Chick, noticing tha a crowd had gathered around them.

"You could've made that suggestion some where else, not in this school hall," replied the principal sharply. "Now go to your classe and don't ever use this corridor, or any place else in this school, for your silly argument again."

That evening, after Chick did his home work, he examined the damaged Ferrari. The best thing to do, he decided, was to buy a new chassis kit and build the Ferrari from scratch There was nothing wrong with the body. I only needed a paint job.

But where would he get the money to pur chase a new kit? He wouldn't dare ask Dad for another cent. Not after what had hap pened. And a kit would cost from five dollar up. He might as well forget the whole thing

He went and sat in the living room, hi

egs sprawled out and his fingers interlaced
across his chest. There wasn't a thing he felt
like doing. He didn't feel like reading. He
didn't feel like playing football. He almost
wished that he had more homework to do, but
that was going too far.

After a minute he realized that he didn't
feel like doing anything except model car
racing.

Dad came in and lightly kicked one of his
sprawled legs. "Hey, what's with you? Your
face is as long as these legs of yours."

Chick shrugged.

"Is it a secret?" his father asked. He crossed
the room and sat on the davenport.

"My car's busted."

"The one you'd just bought from Jack
Harmon?"

Chick nodded.

"Can it be fixed?"

Chick shrugged.

"Well, can it or can't it?"

Chick pulled himself up in the chair and

crossed his left leg over his right. "I suppose
it can. But it'll take an awful lot of work.
Soldering and stuff."

"Let's see the car, Chick."

"You mean what's left of it," said Chick
gloomily. He got the car and held it out to his
father. What was Dad thinking? That he
might put old Humpty Dumpty together
again?

Dad placed the front axle on the brass strips
where old marks showed it had once been
soldered. "We can file this old solder off and
resolder the axle," he suggested. "Know how
the motor fits into the chassis?"

Chick fitted it in the center of the drop arm.
"It goes there," he said. "The metal clip holds
it in place. Just have to mesh the gears. But the
guide's shot, Dad. I've got to have a new one."

"Does Mort Yates sell 'em?"

"Yes."

"Okay. A tiny piece like a guide can't cost
too much." Dad took a coin out of his pocket.
"Here. Go buy one and we'll put this baby
together again."

Chick's eyes brightened like headlights. "You — you mean you're going to help me, Dad?" he asked hopefully.

"Well, I'll do what you can't do yourself. Okay?"

"Why, sure!" Chick swung his arms around Dad's neck, gave him a squeeze that half-choked him, then scrambled to the front door.

"Meowrrrrr!" shrieked Whitey as Chick stepped on the tip of his long white tail.

"Out of my way, Whitey!" Chick shouted as he yanked the door open and flew across the porch and down the steps.

Dad's going to help me! he thought. *He can do the soldering, I'll do the rest. And I'll paint the body, put new decals on it, and put a driver inside and a dashboard and I'll enter it in a Concours d'Elégance!*

He had plenty of paint and decals. And he had a model car driver that had been collecting dust in a drawer for months, just waiting for an opportunity to climb into a cockpit and drive a car. Oh, man! It had turned out to be a pretty good day after all!

5

"Mort — I mean, Mr. Yates — are you going to hold a Concours Saturday?"

Mort nodded. "Saturday afternoon. Then a few Crash-and-Burn races. Why? Got a car you'd like to enter?"

Chick smiled and nodded. He still felt nervous talking with the man who only a few days ago had thrown him out of the place. "Well, I'm fixing up a Ferrari. If I get it finished in time, I'd like to. That is, if . . . if I could."

Mort leaned on the counter, his face hardly six inches away from Chick's. "Okay, Chick. You could. But no fights. Promise?"

Chick laughed. He took back every bad thing he had thought of Mort. "I promise," he said.

"Okay. See you Saturday. Get here early enough to register."

Chick paid for the nylon slot guide. He

started to leave when who should pop into the place but Jack Harmon.

"Well, look who's here," said Jack. "What's up, Chick?"

Chick almost said "None of your business," but caught himself. "I'm fixing up that Ferrari I bought from you," he replied quietly.

"Can I help you? I'd really like to. I mean it."

Chick stared at him. He glanced at Mort, saw him smile. His stomach churned. The last guy in the world he'd want help from was Jack Harmon. Man, what a spot to be in!

He thought about it a second longer, then said, "Okay. I'm going to work on it right now, though." He hoped maybe that would discourage Jack.

It didn't. "Good!" Jack answered.

He looked again at Mort, and Mort winked. "Better help him good, Jack!" he called, as the boys went out the door. "Chick wants to enter the Concours and the race Saturday!"

Jack looked at Chick in surprise. "You do?"

"Yep, I do," answered Chick, and broke into a fast run. He left Jack behind for a couple of seconds before Jack caught up.

Dad and Mom seemed unable to believe their eyes at sight of Jack. He greeted them in that polite way of his, then followed Chick and Mr. Grover downstairs to the basement.

Chick cleaned off the old solder from the metal frame and front axle with steel wool, then fitted the chassis and axle on the chassis jig. Dad had bought the jig for him when he had made his first model car almost two years ago.

Dad plugged in the soldering iron to heat it. He unrolled about six inches of solder from a big roll and dipped the end of it into a can of soldering flux. With a brush he dabbed the areas of the front axle and the curved-up end of the flat metal frame, then held the iron, when it was hot, against the metal frame close to where the two pieces were to join together.

Suddenly the solder melted, flowing between the joints. Dad took the iron away and the solder hardened to a smooth finish almost instantly.

"Gee, Dad! That doesn't look so hard," exclaimed Chick.

"It isn't," agreed Dad. "Just don't put on too much flux, and make sure your iron's good and hot. And keep your fingers away from the hot tip!"

Chick laughed. "Makes sense!" he said.

"Want to solder the axle to the other side?" asked Dad.

"Sure!"

Chick dipped the end of the solder into the flux. Using the brush, he dabbed a little flux near the end of the metal frame that curved up on the left side and on the front axle where the two pieces were to join. He took the soldering iron carefully by its handle and held its tip against the curve of the flat metal strip. He felt jittery.

Suddenly the solder melted and flowed quickly between the joints.

"Okay," said Dad. "Take the iron away."

Chick did. The solder hardened to a neat, smooth finish. Almost as neat as Dad's!

"Hey! Nice work, son," said Dad. "You handle that iron pretty well."

Chick lifted the drop arm and let it drop freely at its pivotal points. It was free as could be. The arm had to work freely so that the pickup brush and the slot flag at its end would keep contact with the track. For good measure, he tightened the small screws on both sides of the chassis mounts a bit more. The pivoting cross bar of the drop arm was fastened to the mounts and these were the only screws that held the drop arm to the chassis.

He noticed something. The axle was sticking out more than a sixteenth of an inch from the left front wheel and was only a thread or two into the right front wheel. Wow! That had to be fixed for sure.

With a wrench he loosened the nut between the right wheel and the nylon bushing, unscrewed the wheel, then did the same thing to the other wheel. He then turned both nuts till they were almost exactly the same distance from the ends of the axle, screwed the wheels back on, tightened the nuts against them and checked the result. He grinned with satisfaction.

"That's a lot better," said Jack over his shoulder. "Funny I hadn't seen it when I had it."

Chick examined the rear wheels. They fitted on the axle well enough. He placed the slot guide on the V-shaped end of the drop arm and tightened a set screw with a tiny allen wrench to hold it. He checked to see if the guide pivoted freely. It did.

He set the motor carefully in place inside the drop arm, fitting the bushing of the front end into the hole in the motor mount that was soldered to a cross bar, and the rear bushing of the motor onto the mount that was cut out in the exact shape to hold it. He pushed the motor down gently, careful to mesh the pinion gear of the motor and the crown gear on the rear axle without stripping the teeth. Then he placed the metal clip over the motor and forced its ends underneath the brass tubing on both sides to secure it.

He turned the rear wheels a little. The gears felt tight. With his allen wrench he loosened the set screw on the crown gear, pulled the gear back slightly, and retightened the screw. He turned the wheels again. The gears meshed smoothly.

He pushed the free end of a green wire, the other end of which was soldered to the lower left-hand post of the motor, through the left-hand hole in the guide and forced a copper pickup brush into a slot at the end of the guide. He stuck the free end of the red wire, the other end of which was soldered to the upper right-hand post of the motor, through a right-hand hole in the guide and forced a second pickup brush into the slot next to the first one. The two brushes held the wires tightly in place.

"Let's see that," said Jack. He took the chassis and brushed out the copper strands smoothly with a small bristle brush. "The brushes will make better contact this way."

He pushed them flat against the bottom of the slot guide unit with the guide sticking down between them.

"Thanks," said Chick. Heck, he knew that. Jack didn't have to tell him. But, then, you can't be sore at a guy for wanting to be helpful.

Chick cleaned the front and rear tires thoroughly by placing drops of model car tire cleaning fluid on a cloth and rubbing it over the tires lightly with his forefinger.

"What're you going to do with the body?" asked Jack, curiously.

Chick picked it up. It was plastic and looked pretty crummy. "I'll get some lighter fluid from Dad, take off the old paint and give it a new paint job. Then I'm going to glue in a seat and a driver."

"Man, you think you can do all that?"

"I'm going to try," said Chick with confidence. "Dad, do you have some lighter fluid?"

"It's upstairs in the cupboard," replied Dad.

Chick ran up the stairs two at a time. Jack followed him. "See you tomorrow, Chick," he said. "I've got to leave."

"Okay. Thanks for helpin'!"

Chick found the fluid, took it to the basement and soaked up a little of it with a piece of cloth. He rubbed the paint on the inside of the body till it was all off, leaving only the clear plastic.

He painted the body with bright red paint, being careful not to get any on the windshield, the side windows or the rear window.

On Friday, after supper, he painted the headlights a bright yellow as well as a ring around the red tail lights. He painted the seams around the doors, the hood, the windows, the rear fenders, the front grille and the parking lights with black India ink. Then across the seams he rubbed a cloth dampened with lighter fluid, leaving a black pin stripe over all the places he had painted.

"It's shaping up beautifully," observed Dad, smiling. "When's the Concours?"

"Tomorrow afternoon."

"Are you going to race it?"

"Sure! But I won't depend much on it. There might be bugs in it and I won't have time to get 'em all out. I'm going to put in my driver and paste on the decals tonight, then try it out on Ken Jason's track tomorrow morning. If there's anything wrong with it I'll fix it then."

"Good!" Dad ruffled his hair. "Go to it, son. And good luck."

"Thanks, Dad."

"I was surprised to see Jack Harmon here last night. Seems like a nice kid."

Chuck shrugged. "Guess he can be if he wants to."

Dad chuckled. "Guess anybody can be if he wants to. Huh, son?"

Chick smiled, and nodded. He knew what Dad meant, all right.

"I don't think you'll need any help from now on," said Dad. "If you do, let me know."

After Dad went upstairs Chick pasted the license decal on the rear first, then the figure six on the hood and doors. Halfway between the doors and the rear fenders he pasted the decals of a white cat, then glued on the dashboard.

He painted the goggles of the driver silver, the jacket light blue, the helmet and gloves black, and left the face its natural flesh color. He painted a bottle cap brown and glued it to the driver's hands when the paint had dried. It passed perfectly for a steering wheel.

He glued the driver to a piece of thin cardboard, then adjusted the cardboard inside the car's body. He secured the cardboard with Scotch tape, then installed strips of fiber glass tape along the bottom of the body shell, inside, for reinforcement, and stuck a pin through the holes. Then he held the car's body away from himself and looked at it, turning it this way and that. Man, it was a dream.

"All I've got to do now is screw the body to the chassis and I'm finished!" he exclaimed proudly.

He waited for the decals to dry. Then he set the chassis inside the body, lined up the mounting holes, inserted the screws and tightened them.

The car was finished!

He rushed up the stairs two at a time, the model car held as if it were an egg.

"Look, Dad! Mom! I've finished my car!"

They were in the living room. Mom looked up from her book and Dad from his magazine.

They looked wide-eyed with pride before any of them said a word.

6

Early Saturday morning Chick called up Ken Jason and asked if he could test his "new" Ferrari on Ken's home track.

"Sure," said Ken. "Bring it over."

On the way to Ken's he met Butch Slade and a couple of other guys.

"Hey! Whose bomb you got?" Butch asked, reaching for Chick's car.

Chick yanked it back. "Mine. Whose you think?"

"Bought it from Mort?"

"No, I didn't buy it from Mort. I repaired the chassis after it busted, then custom-built the body."

Butch laughed. The others joined in, only louder. "I hope you're not going to enter it in the Concours d'Elégance, or the race this afternoon, Chickie, old boy. That bomb will fizzle."

Something like a toothache hit Chick's stomach. "Thanks," he said. "I'm glad you have so much confidence in me, old pal."

He walked away, the guys' laughter roaring in his ears.

Ken liked the Ferrari. "It looks great, Chick! I bet Jack would never recognize it as the one he sold you."

"Know something?" said Chick, smiling. "He helped me customize it!"

Ken's eyes popped. "Well, I'm not too surprised. He's not a bad guy."

Chick shrugged. *Guess everybody thinks he's a good guy but me. But I don't care. I said I'm going to beat the pants off him one of these days and I will.*

Chick placed the Ferrari on the track first — the inside lane — to see how it would run. He placed the flag squarely in the slot, saw that the copper brushes were touching the metal strips properly on each side, then asked Ken to turn on the switch. Chick picked up the controller for the inside lane, pushed the plunger down gently, and the car crawled forward.

A proud smile came over Chick's face. He pushed the plunger father down. The Ferrari picked up speed, slowed at the S-curve, then bolted down the straightaway. It seemed to shimmy a little and sounded noisy.

"Oh, no!" said Chick, the smile fading. "Something's wrong. Maybe it wasn't soldered well enough!"

He stopped the car in front of him, picked it off the track and examined its underside.

The soldered joints were solid. He checked the gears.

"No wonder!" he said. "There's too much play!" But hadn't he adjusted the gears only last night?

Then he saw the trouble. There was at least a thirty-second of play between the bushing and the nut of the right rear wheel!

"I think I've found it, Ken," Chick said hopefully. "Got a wrench?"

"Sure do." Ken got it and handed it to him. Chick loosened the nut between the bushing and the wheel, unscrewed the wheel slightly, then screwed the nut tighter up against the loose bushing. He screwed the wheel back up to the nut, retightened the nut, and checked the gear mesh again.

"Not bad!" he exclaimed with satisfaction. "Let's see how she runs now!"

He placed the Ferrari on the track, the flag in the slot, and picked up the controller.

Ken flicked on the switch. Chick pushed the plunger down gently, letting the Ferrari take off slowly. Gradually he gave it more power by pressing down farther on the plunger. The car swung around the S-curve, sped down the straightaway, shot around the U and then screamed down the stretch in front of him. He sent it around the track twice. The shimmy was gone. The grating noise was gone.

"I think I've got me a real bomb, Ken," he said, a wide smile on his face. "Let's race."

They conducted a five-minute Wildcat race, using a mechanical timer.

Ken's Ford GTP was ahead at the end of the first lap. Chick, anxious to catch up, gave the Ferrari full throttle on the long stretch, pushing the plunger down as far as it would go. Thumbing off just before it reached the U-curve, he gunned it, thumbed off and gunned it again as it came around the bend. Too fast. The Ferrari spun out and sat still, its flag out of the slot.

He straightened the car, slotted the flag, and full-throttled the Ferrari down the long stretch toward the S-curve. As it sped in front of him it clicked the score marker to 2. The marker on the opposite side read 3. A second later it read 4 as the Ford finished another lap.

On Chick's sixth lap he thumbed off too late at the S-curve, and the Ferrari sailed over the fence and crashed to the floor.

"Track!" he yelled, filled with horror.

He picked up the car, examined it carefully, and grinned with relief. "It's okay!" he shouted.

At the sound of the bell the race stopped and the boys checked their scores. Ken's Ford GTP had finished with fifty-five laps, Chick's with forty-six.

"Man, I'm lousy," said Chick. "You'd think I'd never raced before."

"Well, it's the first time you've raced that bomb," said Ken. "What do you expect?"

"Better than that score, that's what," re-replied Chick determinedly.

At one o'clock Chick and Ken registered their cars at *Mort's Pit Stop* and paid their entrance fees. Mort Yates himself inspected the cars for length, weight and other technical specifications. Then Eddie Lane, Mort's assistant, placed the cars on the long shelf among the other beautiful cars already there. By one-thirty, judging time for the Concours d'Elégance, there were eleven cars entered in the contest, including Jack Harmon's yellow Lola T-70, Butch's black Porsche and Ken's two-toned black and yellow Ford GTP.

Eddie Lane was the judge. He looked at each car and wrote down points on a scoring sheet. Awards were made by the number of points a car accumulated. The most points it could get were thirty.

There were lots of things a judge looked and gave points for. General appearance, for example. Cleanliness. Did the car have a driver? Was he painted and in detail? Was there a steering wheel? An instrument panel? Exhaust pipes?

Exhaust pipes? Chick's heart fluttered. His red Ferrari didn't have them. Few of the cars did. Would not having them ruin his chances?

At last it was over. Eddie Lane checked the score sheet. Then he climbed up to the platform and spoke into the microphone.

"Attention, everybody! The cars have been judged in the Concours d'Elégance and the top three winners chosen. These were judged on their general appearance, craftsmanship, and special ingenuity in making and installing the different accessories."

He cleared his throat. "Third prize — a blue ribbon and a set of trackside figures — to Mike Kotmel!"

A roar resounded through the big room.

"Second prize — a red ribbon and a clear plastic Marauder body — to Duane Chrisman!"

Another roar resounded. Then silence.

"First prize — a white ribbon and a brass tube frame — to Chick Grover!"

"Yaaaaay!"

"Congratulations, Chick!"

Chick stood, almost paralyzed. He was looking at Eddie Lane and Eddie was looking at him and smiling. "Here you are, Chick," he said, holding out the ribbon and the prize. "Come and get it."

Chick broke out of the spell, stepped forward and accepted the ribbon and prize. "Th-thanks," he said.

When he turned, Butch and Jack were waiting for him with outstretched hands. "Guess I don't know what it takes to be a winner," said Butch. "That's why I never win a Concours."

"You sure turned my old heap into a beauty, Chick," said Jack. "I'm glad it won."

"Thanks, guys," said Chick proudly.

He entered the first two-minute Crash-and-Burn race with Ken, Butch, Jack and four other guys — including fellows much older. Since there were only eight lanes on the track, not all the entries were able to race at the same time. The winner would race the three remaining cars.

Chick gooped the Ferrari's rear tires on Butch's goop pad, set the car on the Number 4 blue lane which was assigned to him, then waited for the count from Eddie Lane, the race director. Jack's Lola T-70 was on the red lane on his right and Butch's black Porsche on his left. Somehow he wished Jack's car were in another lane.

The race drivers started with their thumbs down on the controllers. At the count of "Three!" the race director turned on the switch and the race was on.

Chick kept the Ferrari at full throttle down the long straightaway and was careful as could be at the curves and bends. One deslotment in a Crash-and-Burn and you were eliminated.

He eased around the curves, noticing other cars speeding by him. But he ignored them. Two years of slot car racing had taught him never to look at the other cars. You had to watch your own. It was often at that fraction of a second, when you took your eyes off your car, when it would spin out or deslot.

One car stalled before it completed its first lap, eliminating it from the race. Another spun out on its second lap. Down the straightaway, around the bend, under the overhead, up and around the S-bend, down the long stretch near the wall in back, then the wide banking U-curve, the sweeper, that led once again into the long straightaway. Around and around they raced, the best drivers — and the luckiest ones — staying in there.

"One minute's up!" announced the race director.

Chick's hopes climbed. He was still in there. So were Ken, Butch and Jack.

"Track!" someone yelled. The power was shut off. The cars stopped dead. And Chick saw that Ken's Ford GTP had overshot the sweeper and gone sailing off into space and to the floor.

Five cars left on the track. Chick felt his pulse speed up as the race started again. The controller was hot in his hand. Hot and wet from his sweating palm.

Stay in there, you little red bomb! he pleaded. *Stay in there!*

Then it happened. On the sharp S-curve past the overhead at the left side of the track.

The red Ferrari was making the sharp turn when up from its right side a yellow Lola T-70 came bursting at breakneck speed. Its tail spun out just enough to hit the Ferrari's nose, de-slotting the flag.

Chick jerked his thumb up but it was too late to save the Ferrari. It skidded over the lanes, crashed against the high wall and shuddered to a dead stop.

"You — you —!" Chick glared at Jack Harmon. "You nerfed me! You nerfed me on purpose!"

7

Chick drew back his fist, but Ken grabbed his arm. "Hold it, Chick, or Mort will throw you out for good."

Jack's attention was on the Lola T-70 speeding around the track.

"It was an accident!" he said. "I didn't mean to nerf you!"

"Like heck you didn't!"

Someone came and stood at Chick's elbow. Someone big and authoritative. "Just let me see your shadow get into a scrap and you won't race her again, Chick," came Mort Yates's stern warning.

Chick looked up at him. "But he nerfed me, Mort!"

"There's no law that says you can't," said Mort. "Why don't you try nerfing him?"

"Because I don't like it, that's why," answered Chick hotly.

"I said I didn't do it on purpose," insisted Jack, the Lola T-70 still under his complete control. "Can't we drop it there?"

Just then Butch's black Porsche spun out on the sweeper and lay still. "For crying out loud, you guys!" he yelled. "Why don't you keep your traps shut?"

The Porsche was out of the race too. Butch picked it up, shooting an angry look at Mort and Chick.

Chick managed to control his tongue and

temper and hung around until the race was over. Jack's car had won the first race, and then had won over the other three drivers, too.

Butch snapped at Chick outdoors, catching Chick by surprise. "You're always shooting off your mouth, Chick. Why couldn't you have waited till you were outside? I had a hot race going."

"Oh, yeah? How about me? What would you do if Harmon had nerfed *your* car?"

"I don't know. But I wouldn't have yelled my head off like you did and thrown all the drivers off. Man!"

Chick clamped his lips and ran down the street. He expected — hoped — that Butch would yell for him to slow down, but Butch didn't. A lump rose and stuck in his throat.

He almost bumped into Police Officer Tom Duffy as he rounded the corner onto Carbon Street. "Hey, watch it!" Tom yelled, holding out a ham-sized hand.

"Oh, sorry, Mr. Duffy."

"What happened? Get into another scrap?"

There you go. You didn't even have to tell people any more.

"Guess so," said Chick, catching his breath. "Guess all I do is get into scraps."

"Jack Harmon again?"

Chick nodded and explained what had happened. He also told about Butch.

"Don't worry too much about either of them," advised Mr. Duffy. "I know both boys just as well as you do. And I know you too, Chick. You can't take a ribbing. You fly off the handle like an angry hornet when you're picked on. That's why they pick on you. They enjoy seeing you get hot under the collar. The only thing to do is learn to take it. Show 'em you're not bothered by their foolishness. Before long they'll get tired of sticking those pins into you."

Chick walked the rest of the way home, feeling a lot better. Guess policemen like Tom Duffy were made especially for kids like himself.

In math class the following day Mr. Woodrow gave a fifteen-minute speed test. It was, in Chick's opinion, tough. He skipped some problems, guessed at others. He was finished in ten minutes and spent the rest of the time drawing a racing car. It was low-slung, with narrow round wheels in front and wide flat ones in back.

After the papers were handed in Chick put the drawing away. He finished it in history class, adding the driver, the circled numbers and the windshield wipers. It was pretty snazzy, he thought.

Mr. Woodrow returned the corrected papers on Tuesday. Chick hated to look at the grade, but Mr. Woodrow's blunt forefinger directed his eyes to it: 49.

"It's not quite, but almost, the lowest mark in class, Chick," announced Mr. Woodrow not too kindly. "I want you to study that chapter of problems again, then do the test over."

Chick looked up. "You mean you're giving me a chance to get a better mark?"

"Not at all, my boy. What I want is for you to do them all over again, but with one difference: They're to be one-hundred percent correct. Do you understand that, Chick?"

Chick gulped and looked away. "I understand," he said.

He was aware of every student in the room looking at him. One pair of eyes, in particular, drew his attention. The taunting, teasing eyes of Jack Harmon.

Chick remembered Mr. Duffy's words of wisdom. Sure, he felt like giving Jack a dirty look back, but he wasn't going to. He'd ignore Jack completely. He owed Mr. Duffy that much, to give his words of wisdom a chance to work.

8

"How about a race at Mort's in half an hour?" asked Ken Jason. "I'd like to try out my Cooper Ford."

"Fine," said Jack. "How about it, Chick? It'll give you a chance to even up on me. Or are you afraid I'll nerf you?"

The skin on Chick's neck crawled. "You did nerf me on purpose, didn't you?"

"No, I didn't. I told you that. What you can't seem to get through your thick skull, Chick Grover, is that my Lola T-70 can hold the track around curves better than almost any car around."

They got their cars and went to *Mort's Pit Stop*. Only three guys were racing their cars. Jack asked Mort if he and Ken and Chick could run a Crash-and-Burn. Sure, said Mort, as soon as the other three guys were finished.

About seven minutes later the track was clear. Ken, Chick and Jack paid their fee. Eddie Lane agreed to act as race director. The boys gave their cars a once-around-the-track trial run, then set them on the starting line.

Jack had No. 3, the orange lane; Ken, No. 5, the red lane; Chick, No. 7, the yellow lane.

"Thumbs down!" announced Eddie Lane.

The boys pushed down their controller

plungers. Eddie counted, "One! Two! Three!," yanked the switch, and the cars took off as if shot from rifles. They reached the first hairpin curve almost at the same time, Chick thumbing off and on to slow the Ferrari. The cars sped to the second curve, left again to the underpass, then right on the straightaway next to the wall. Ken's Cooper Ford edged out Jack's Lola and Chick's Ferrari as the cars reached the sweeper at the right.

The Cooper Ford led at the finish of the first lap. The Lola was second, the Ferrari third. Chick kept the plunger down as the Ferrari zipped to the first hairpin, then thumbed up and down, up and down, to slow the little red car. He full-throttled it again as it headed for the next curve. Up on the plunger. Down again. The Ferrari swept past the Lola and came up even with the Cooper as they swept around the wide bend. Thumb all the way down, the Ferrari dashed past the Cooper and into the lead.

Caution forced Chick to thumb off again

at the first hairpin. He did it just in time. The rear of the Ferrari whipped around slightly and would have spun out if he had waited an instant longer. As it was, the rear tires spun briefly before traction took hold and the little racer was on its way again. Chick held his breath. A stall would've meant elimination.

The slowdown gave Jack and Ken the chance to pass Chick. The Lola T-70 and the Cooper Ford were almost body to body as they roared around the sweeper. The Lola took the lead as the car finished their third lap.

Chick full-throttled the Ferrari around the wide bend and the straightaway, eased briefly on the hairpin, full-throttled again, eased on the second curve, then shot the Ferrari up to the underpass, letting up at the last instant. The Ferrari made the turn all right, then sped down the upper straightaway, passing the Cooper Ford and catching up with the Lola T-70 at the wide bend.

It kept the lead for the next three laps, going into the eighth section when the race director called out: "One minute! Yellow, seven laps, eight sections! Orange, seven laps, two! Red, six laps, eighteen!"

Chick hid a pleased grin. Six sections ahead of Jack wasn't too safe a lead. Jack could make good time on the sharp curves and be way ahead of him before the two minutes were up.

Chick kept the Ferrari at full throttle as it roared down the upper straightaway and whipped around the sweeper. It zipped past him, ending the eighth lap.

Seconds later it ended the ninth lap, almost ten sections ahead of the Lola and a full lap ahead of the Cooper Ford.

Chick was ahead of Jack by fifteen sections at the end of the tenth lap. He grinned as he breezed the Ferrari around the two sharp curves and then through the underpass. He had it made now. The Lola was lost in his dust. It could hold the track at sharp curves better than most cars around? What a laugh!

"Thirty seconds!" announced Eddie Lane.

Chick full-throttled the Ferrari down the upper straightaway and into the steep bend. He passed Ken's Cooper Ford, placing it two laps behind his Ferrari. What's happened to Ken? wondered Chick.

Man, am I hot! I can make that little red Ferrari do anything I want it to!

The car finished the eleventh lap. Just a few seconds left, thought Chick. A few seconds . . .

Be careful going around the curve. Ease up a little. Now down to the next curve. Ease up again. There. Now full-throttle it. That's it. Watch it! You're at the underpass! Thumb off! Thumb off! You're going too fast! Too fast!

The Ferrari spun out. Stalled.

"Oh, no!" cried Chick, cupping his head between his hands.

Jack Harmon won.

9

On Tuesday, after school, Ken invited Chick to race on his home track. Chick cleaned the tires of the Ferrari first with oil of wintergreen, smoothed the brushes, then he and Ken ran their racers a few laps to warm them up.

"Let's run a Crash-and-Burn for two minutes," suggested Ken.

"Okay."

They lined up the racers — Chick his Ferrari and Ken his Ford GTP. Ken set the timer and at his count of "Three!" the cars took off. Chick full-throttled the Ferrari down to the first curve, eased up sharply, then sent it whirring down the long stretch, its rear end vibrating as if it tried to shake something off. Chick frowned. Now what?

He thumbed off and on at the doughnut curve, but too late. The flag deslotted.

Chick examined the tires again and found a cinder lodged on the right rear tire. He wiped it off.

"Say," said Ken, "a week from Saturday Mort is holding a Concours d'Elégance, then Semi and Main racing events. Want to sign up?"

"Sure. Why not?"

Ken reset the timer and the boys started to race again. This time the little red Ferrari roared down the track with barely a shimmy. Ken led in the first two laps by inches, then crept steadily ahead. Chick tried to catch him on the straightaways but wasn't able to. Neither could he gain on the curves. Ken knew what his car could do on these curves and used his knowledge to the hilt.

When the timer banged at the end of the two minutes, Ken's Ford GTP had completed twenty-six laps to the Ferrari's twenty-two.

"Let's race again," said Chick. "Make it five minutes this time."

"Okay."

This time Chick did better but Ken still won, sixty-one laps to Chick's fifty-seven.

"You going to enter the Ferrari in the Concours again?" asked Ken.

"I don't think it's got much of a chance now," said Chick truthfully. "It's pretty banged up again."

Ken took a low, sleek body with curved

fenders, headlights, tail lights and long rain-drop roof off a shelf. The blue paint was partly scratched off. The number on its sides was 8.

"You can have it," he said. "It's been sitting here collecting dust. It needs a new paint job and a driver and, of course," he added, smiling, "a chassis, and motor!"

"What make body is it?"

"A Stingray. And it's 1/24th scale."

Chick took it. "Thanks, Ken. You sure you don't want anything for it?"

"I said I'm giving it to you, didn't I?"

Chick grinned. "Yes, you did."

On his way home he met Butch Slade. He and Butch hadn't said more than a dozen words to each other in the last week. That silly argument had created a void in his life, left a hole so big he didn't know what he could do to close it again. He had missed Butch. They'd been buddies as long as he could remember.

"Hi," said Butch. "You still sore?"

Chick stared in surprise. "Sore? Heck, no. Why should I be sore?"

Butch shrugged and grinned a small grin. "Are you going to enter the events at Mort's a week from Saturday? He's giving some good prizes. You can have a chance to build up your equipment."

"I think so. Matter of fact, see this?" Chick held up the shell of the Stingray. "I'm going to dress up this bomb, put a chassis in it and enter it in the Concours."

"Man, you have a lot of dressing up to do on that one."

"I know. But I'm going to do it, anyway. I've got that brass tube frame that I won and I'll use the motor from the Ferrari. It'll be almost like a second car."

"More like a first!" Butch laughed. "Well, good luck."

They parted and Chick felt much happier. How do you like that? Neither had to apologize to the other. They were friends again, just like that.

10

The next evening Chick began soldering the pieces for the chassis in the basement. A week from Saturday were the Heat Races, the Semifinals and the Main events. A week from Saturday!

He began to sweat and had trouble holding the tip of the soldering iron on the joints. He put down the strip of solder he had cut from the spool and wiped his forehead. He'd never get the car done in time to enter it in the Concours and Semis. Never!

He felt like giving up then and there. There would be other Concourses. Other races with prizes.

He set the iron aside, pressed his fists tightly against his eyes and swallowed hard. His left elbow struck the soldering iron and knocked it off the table. It banged against the leg of the bench and fell to the floor.

He picked it up and heard footsteps on the stairs. Who was it? Mom? Dad?

"What fell, Chick?"

It was Dad.

"The — the soldering iron."

Dad came beside him. Chick was holding the iron and strip of solder above the joint he wanted to solder.

"You've been down here quite some time," Dad said. "What have you done so far?"

For a second or two Chick was quiet. Then he answered, "Nothing."

"That's what I thought. What do you have to do?"

Chick told him. "But I can do it," he added hastily. "You don't have to —"

"What do you want soldered, Chick?" interrupted Dad.

Chick swallowed, then explained. Dad soldered the pieces of the chassis and secured the motor while Chick painted the body a royal blue and the white circle and figure 8 with their respective colors.

The next night, while Dad worked on the axles and wheels, Chick drew an instrument panel on a file card and painted it. Then he cut two small pieces of wire and dabbed one end of each with cement and fitted both of them to the windshield. By now the paint on the file card was dry. He cut out the instrument panel and glued it in place.

"Wipers and instrument panel," said his father, smiling. "A nice touch. The chassis's all ready, Chick."

Chick fitted the body to it, then set the finished model on the bench.

"A beauty, son," said Dad. "Keep this up and you'll wind up being an automobile designer."

Chick laughed. "They make a lot of money, Dad?"

Dad chuckled. "More than a clerk like myself."

The next evening he put the revamped Stingray through its paces at *Mort's Pit Stop*. Dad was with him.

"Only fifteen laps," said Chick in disappointment after a two-minute trial run. "That's not enough. It has to do at least eighteen or it won't have a chance."

"What can we do?"

"Rewind the motor. But I don't know how . . ."

"That'll increase its gear ratio, won't it? I'll help you."

Dad rewound the motor. The next day they took the Stingray back to Mort's. This time the Stingray hit eighteen laps and three sections.

"It's coming, Dad," Chick said triumphantly.

On Friday, the day before the races, he and Ken went to *Mort's Pit Stop*, registered, paid their entry fees and had their cars inspected. Mort himself inspected them.

"Going to enter your cars in the Concours?" he asked.

"Yes," replied Chick.

"Then you'd better be here early. The Concours starts at one-thirty sharp."

"We'll be here," said Chick.

They read the Model Car Racing announcement before leaving.

MODEL CAR RACING

SATURDAY, NOV. 16

1:30 P.M. CONCOURS D'ELEGANCE

1st Prize:	White ribbon and model car kit
2nd Prize:	Red ribbon and deluxe controller
3rd, 4th & 5th Prizes:	Blue ribbons designating place won in contest

2:00 P.M. HEAT RACE

First 6 winners:	Ribbons and right to compete in Main Event. Balance of drivers to race in consolation races according to performance.

2:30 P.M. FIRST CONSOLATION RACE

Ribbons to first 2 winners

3:00 P.M. SECOND CONSOLATION RACE

Ribbons to first 2 winners

3:30 P.M. SEMI-MAIN EVENT

Ribbons to first 2 winners

4:00 P.M. MAIN EVENT

1st Prize: Trophy plus $10 in merchandise
2nd Prize: Ribbon plus $5 in merchandise
3rd Prize: Ribbon plus $2 in merchandise
4th Prize: $1.00 Track time
5th Prize: $ .75 Track time

CLASS OF CARS

No Limitation

"They're pretty good prizes," observed Ken.

"I'll say." Chick's pulse was already speeding up.

11

The Concours d'Elégance was on.

There were twenty-three cars entered, all lined up at an angle and side by side on a shelf by the wall left of the raceway. Eddie Lane was judge, as before. Each boy with a car in the Concours waited breathlessly.

Mine won't win, thought Chick, his hands clasped tightly behind him. *There are too many that are more good-looking.* That bright shiny red Lola GT, for example. That Mako Shark II with Firestone lettered on the tires. And that sharp, forest-green Camaro with the chrome door handles and silver bumpers. They're terrific.

The judge added up the scores. At last he picked up the blue ribbons. Chick breathed ever so slowly. The fifth prize went to the Mako Shark II. The fourth prize to a green Rover BRM. The third prize . . . Chick breathed easier now. There was no use being anxious. His Stingray had no chance. The third prize went to an orange Ferrari. The second prize, a red ribbon . . . Chick's heart pounded like a hammer gone crazy. *The judge was putting it on his Stingray!*

Someone — Ken — slapped him on the shoulder. "Chick! You won second prize! A deluxe controller!"

Chick was dazed.

The first prize went to the Camaro with the chrome door handles.

"Nice going, Chick," said Jack Harmon, whose entry was a pink Chaparral. "That's the second time you've won a prize in a Concours. Well, let's see what your bomb can do in the Heat!"

Don't sass him back, thought Chick. *Don't let him get your goat. Remember the wise words of Mr. Duffy.*

At three minutes of two Eddie Lane made an announcement. "Attention, racers! The Heat Race will begin in exactly three minutes.

It will last for two minutes. There are twenty-three entries. The six drivers who complete the most laps in the two minutes are qualified to enter the Main Event. Drivers who place eighteenth through twenty-third will compete in the First Consolation Race. The first two winners in that race will then compete in the Second Consolation Race. The other four are eliminated.

"Drivers who place thirteenth through seventeenth will compete in the Second Consolation Race with the two winners of the First Consolation Race. The first two winners in this race will compete in the Semi-Main Event. The other five drivers are eliminated. Drivers who place seventh through twelfth in the Heat Race will also compete in the Semi-Main Event. The first two winners in the Semi-Main Event will compete in the Main Event. The remaining five are eliminated.

"I'll call off your names in the order that you've registered. Choose your lane, take two practice laps, then wait at the starting line. Number One, Dick Ealy. Number Two, Jack Harmon. Number Three, Harry Mills . . ."

Eddie called off eight names. Chick's wasn't one of them. After the eight drivers raced, eight more would be called and then the remaining seven for the Heat Race.

Color stickers, matching the lanes for identification, were put on the cars. Then the cars were lined up. Jack's was in the yellow lane, Number 7. Four turn marshals were in their positions at the corners.

"Okay," said Eddie. "At the count of three! Thumbs down! One! Two! Three!"

Eddie switched on the power and the cars took off. They streaked to the first hairpin curve, slowed briefly, their tails whipping out ever so slightly. A black Lola 40 scrambled into the lead going into the second curve, followed by two Ferraris, and Jack Harmon's Chaparral fourth. For two laps there was little change. Then the Chaparral moved up into third position and held the spot for five laps.

Suddenly one of the Ferraris spun out at the dangerous S-curve at the underpass. An instant later, just as the turn marshal shouted "Track!," the car in the next lane struck the spunout racer and deslotted.

The turn marshal placed the cars quickly back on the tracks. At the count of "Three!" the race continued. The black Lola held the lead for the next four laps, creeping steadily ahead. A Ferrari was in second place, Jack Harmon's Chaparral in third.

At the end of a minute the black Lola had covered ten laps, the Ferrari nine and Jack's Chaparral eight laps and ten sections.

Jack's Chaparral crept ahead, gaining at the curves. The seconds ticked off slowly while the cars gobbled up the sections.

"Time's up!" Eddie Lane yelled. "Don't touch your cars till I get their laps recorded!"

A Ferrari 250 GTO came in first with nineteen laps, four sections. Jack Harmon's Chaparral came in second with eighteen laps, seventeen sections.

Seconds later Eddie had them recorded, then called off the names of the next eight drivers. Chick waited breathlessly. At last: "Number Six, Chick Grover. Number Seven, Kenneth Jason. Number Eight —"

Chick chose the orange lane, Number 3. Ken, the green lane, Number 2. They put color stickers on their cars. The drivers took two trial laps each, then the race began.

Chick's hand was warm on the controller, his thumb pressing the plunger way down as the royal blue Stingray shot for the first curve. Up on the plunger. Down again on the short straightaway. Up again as the car approached the second turn. The tail whipped slightly as the Stingray burst across the stretch to the underpass, slowed briefly as it negotiated the S-curve, then shot like a blue streak down the long stretch near the wall to the sweeper. Down it came and breezed like a bullet in front of Chick to complete its first lap.

A racer spun out on its second lap. Another deslotted and roared over the tracks, tumbling over the side to the floor as it tried to take the inside curve of the steep, wide bend too fast.

Seconds later the racer in the white lane spun out on the first S-curve. The car in the purple lane stalled almost in the same section. At the end of the Heat Race the car in the blue lane came in first with eighteen laps, three sections; the car in the purple lane seventeen laps, eight sections; Chick's car in the orange lane seventeen laps, two sections; Ken's car in the green lane sixteen laps, eight sections; the car in the yellow lane sixteen laps, four sections and the car in the black lane fifteen laps, one section.

All of the last seven cars finished the Heat. Eddie Lane tallied the points. Chick and Ken waited anxiously.

"Beat you by a lap and a half," said a voice at Chick's elbow.

Chick stiffened. "So what? That was just the Heat."

Jack Harmon chuckled. "I know. I never do as well as I can in Heats. I'm best in Semis or Mains, where it really counts."

The braggart, thought Chick coldly.

"Attention!" Eddie's booming voice over the loudspeaker silenced the room. "The six winners of the Heat Race eligible to compete in the Main Event are: Number one, James Sand. Number two, Paul Miller. Number three, Kim Norman. Number four, Frank Spry. Number five, Jack Harmon. Number six, Bob Sobus."

A fist poked Chick gently in the ribs. "Well, how about that? I don't have to worry about the consolation races!"

Chick turned grim eyes at Jack Harmon. "And I don't have to worry about being nerfed."

Too late. The one thing he didn't want to do anymore was sass. Jack Harmon, in particular. Jack could rattle him to pieces. And when you're racing model cars you can't be rattled or you're sunk. You can't think of anything else. You can't think of how many laps you're behind or ahead of the other guy or you'll lose for sure.

"Guess you'll never get it through your fat

head that I wouldn't nerf you on purpose, will you?" said Jack.

Chick didn't answer.

He and Ken placed fourteenth and sixteenth respectively, qualifying them in the Second Consolation Race. Butch Slade's black Porsche came in eighteenth.

12

The drivers in the First Consolation Race who had finished eighteenth through twenty-third in the Heat Races selected lanes and put color stickers on their cars. Each car took its two trial laps, then lined up at the starting line.

"Okay!" said race director Eddie Lane. "The first driver to cross the finish line after twenty laps wins first place! The next car in line wins second place! The others are eliminated! Get ready!"

The power was switched on and the cars

took off. A red Mustang took the lead immediately. It shot to the first hairpin, slowed ever so briefly, shot to the next hairpin, slowed again, then blazed across the longer stretch to the underpass. A Barracuda was second, a Porsche third, a blue Ferrari fourth. A Ford GTP and a Lola T-70 trailed.

The Mustang led the pack across the long straightaway near the wall. At the steep bank Butch's black Porsche caught up. The cars remained tire to tire as they blazed across the starting line to complete lap one.

The Mustang pulled ahead after the first sharp curve, slithered to the second. Then, just as it slowed to make the turn, its tail spun out and the car stopped! But only for a second. The fat rear wheels spun, found traction and the car took off again. But that second was enough for Butch's Porsche to pull into the lead.

It stayed in the lead for five laps.

Then — a surprise. The blue Ferrari blazed

by the Porsche down the sweeper and sprang into the lead! It held it for two laps then was overtaken by the Mustang.

Come on, Butch! breathed Chick.

The Porsche was less than half a section behind the Ferrari as it whipped through the underpass then blasted across the straightaway. It caught up with the Ferrari at the sweeper, went ahead momentarily, then trailed again. It remained third to the seventeenth lap, just two sections behind the Ferrari and about half a lap behind the Mustang.

In the eighteenth lap the Porsche did it. It came up even with the Ferrari, edged by it as both cars made the first sharp curve, stayed ahead going into the second and during the short stretch to the underpass. *Watch it here, Butch!*

The Porsche hung in there. It was ahead by two sections as it completed its nineteenth lap.

The horn buzzed. The cars stopped. The Mustang was first to complete the twenty laps. In second place was Butch Slade's Porsche.

The cars that had placed thirteenth through seventeenth in the Heat Race competed in the Second Consolation Race with the two winners of the First Consolation Race.

The place winners, beginning with the thirteenth, chose their lanes. A gold Dodge Charger was in the black, Chick's Stingray in the yellow, a red Firebird in the purple, Ken Jason's Ford GTP in the red, the Mustang in the blue, Butch Slade's Porsche in the orange and a Lola 40 in the green.

"Thumbs down!" The Second Consolation Race was on.

The cars took off together as the power was turned on. Chick was filled with excitement and fear, fear of spinning out and thus losing ground. He tried to shake it off, to remain as calm as he could, to think only of the Stingray as it zipped from one curve to the other, skimmed like bolt lightning across the straightaways, and glided down the sweeper.

One lap. Two. Three.

Suddenly the red Firebird spun out at the underpass.

"Track!" a turn marshal shouted.

The cars stopped for a couple of seconds as the car was straightened and its flag re-slotted.

Five laps. Six. Seven. On and on . . . Only two could win. Only two would enter in the Semi-Main Event.

Chick felt as if the room were closing in on him. The controller was like a hot iron in his hand as he watched his little Stingray take the corners ever so beautifully and slither like a blue streak down the stretches.

What lap was it now? Eleventh? Twelfth? It seemed so long ago when they had started. Where was the Dodge Charger? He seemed to remember gliding past it around the wide bend. He wasn't sure. How were Ken and Butch doing?

No! his mind shouted at him. Don't think of the others!

Suddenly the yell: "Twenty laps!"

The cars stopped. Everyone looked anxiously at the race director.

"The winner: black lane!"

It was the gold Dodge Charger. The owner jumped happily and whooped like an Indian. Then silence.

"Number two winner: yellow lane!"

Someone yelled in Chick's ears and pounded him on the back. "Chick! You won second place!"

He was so choked he couldn't speak. He stretched and unstretched his fingers, then wiped his sweating forehead. He had crossed the second hurdle. The next would be stiffer.

13

"Sorry, Butch," said Chick.

Butch shrugged. "So am I. But we both can't win."

"You did okay, Chick," said Jack Harmon. "But the Semi is tougher. You're up against real tough bombs in that one. But, of course, you know that. You're getting to be a champ."

Chick's face turned iron-hot. He clenched his fist and then unclenched it. He knew Jack wanted him to get rattled. Jack figured that if Chick got rattled he'd blow up and lose the race.

Chick forced a smile. "I'll do the best I can."

"Get ready for the Semi!" yelled the race director.

The drivers who had placed seventh through twelfth chose their lanes. The boy with the Dodge Charger chose the green lane, leaving the remaining white outside lane to Chick.

"This will be fifty laps!" the race director announced. "The first car to finish is winner. The next car with the most number of laps is second place winner. Both winners will then compete in the Main Event. All right. At the count of three. Thumbs down! One! Two! Three!"

The race was on.

The red Porsche 904 in the purple lane took
the lead going into the hairpin and held it going into the second curve. A blue Lola T-70
gained on it as all eight cars streaked toward
the underpass. All eight made the sharp S-
curve, tore down the long straightaway and
down the sweeper. The Porsche was first to
finish the first lap, the Lola T-70 second, the
Dodge Charger third, and Chick's Stingray
fourth.

Round and round . . .

Chick's thumb trembled on the plunger as
he pressed it down to full-throttle the Stingray on the stretches. *Rrrrrrrrrr!* Eight motors
roared as one as the racers swarmed down the
sweeper, eating up the sections and then the
laps.

The Stingray pulled ahead of the Charger.
It gained on the red Porsche. The Ferrari
275P whizzed by it at the underpass, threaten-
ing to catch up with the Porsche. Chick full-
throttled the Stingray down the long straight,
held it full speed on the sweeper. It was gaining . . . gaining . . .

Three laps later it overtook the Ferrari. Round and round . . . Round and round . . .

"Thirty laps!" yelled the Race Director.

Round and round . . .

"Forty laps!"

"Forty-five!"

The controller was hot in Chick's hand. Which position was he in? The Third? Fourth? Fifth?

Round and round . . .

And then the shout: "FIFTY LAPS!" The cars stopped. Gently, Chick lay the controller aside and stretched his tension-gripped fingers. And waited.

"The winner, Ted Curit's Ferrari 275P! Second place winner, Chick Grover's Stingray!"

Chick gulped.

"Well, you came through again, champ!" cried Jack Harmon. "Let's see what you can do in the Main!"

Chick dabbed drops of oil of wintergreen

on the rear tires of the Stingray in readiness for the last race, drank a glass of orange juice with Ken and Butch, and rested.

"Thumbs down! One! Two! Three!"

The Main Event was on. Two hundred laps. This was the big one. The real big one. *Rrrrrrrr!* Motors roared. Sparks flickered as all eight cars took off at the same time.

Watch your car carefully! Concentrate every second!

Round and round . . .

The Stingray, a Cheetah Riverside and a Porsche 904 hung together down the stretches and the curves as if a stiff wire were drawn through them. A gray Alfa Romeo in the white lane crept slowly ahead. A Ford GT in the red lane and a Lola 40 in the purple were a couple of sections ahead. The Ferrari 250 GTO and Jack Harmon's Chaparral were fighting for the lead.

Round and round and round . . .

The Alfa Romeo deslotted at the sweeper and went sailing over the track to the floor.

"Track!" shouted a turn marshal.

The power was shut off. The car put back on the track. The power turned on.

"Lane eight, twenty-five laps," called the race director. "Lane seven, twenty-four. Lane six, twenty-four. Lane five, twenty-two. Lane four, twenty-three. Lane three, twenty-three. Lane two, twenty-three. Lane one, twenty-one."

Lane three, twenty-three. *That's me!* thought Chick. *That's my Stingray!*

The Ferrari spun out at the underpass. "Track!"

Round and round . . .

And then, at the first hairpin, the Stingray spun out.

"Track!"

"Oh, no!" cried Chick.

The spinout helped the other cars to gain at least a section or two on him. He had to gain them back, and more.

"Thumbs down! One! Two! Three!"

Chick tried to concentrate on the race now more than ever. The controller was like a

torch in his sweating hand. Sweat beaded his forehead, dripped into his eyes. He wiped it away.

"Car in lane four completes fifty laps," announced the race director. "Lane eight, forty-eight. Lane seven, forty-seven. Lane six, forty-five. Lane five, forty-three. Lane three, forty-five. Lane two, forty-four. Lane one, forty-nine."

Lane seven, forty-seven laps. That's Jack Harmon's, thought Chick. And I've got forty-five. *Come on, Stingie! Watch the curve! Up with the thumb! Now down! That's it! Thumb up again! That second curve comes awfully fast. Pump the plunger! Down with the thumb to the underpass! Up! Down again around the S! Watch that tail! Don't let it spin out!*

There! Made it! Down the long straight-away along the wall. Then the sweeper. Keep it down! Down! Was that a green Ford you passed? Never mind! Keep going, and keep your eyes open.

Round and round . . .

One hundred laps . . .

". . . lane seven, ninety-four!"

". . . lane three, ninety-two!"

Chick heard the other announcements but he was mostly interested in those two. Jack Harmon's and his.

One hundred and fifty laps . . .

". . . lane seven, one hundred and forty-five!" Jack's gained a little! ". . . lane three, one hundered and forty-four!"

One lap behind!

Round and round . . .

A car spun out at the sweeper and went tumbling over the side. "Track!" A momentary delay as a turn marshal went to pick it up. The white sticker on it read 1. It was one of the leaders.

"Too bad," said the turn marshal. "Motor's busted."

Round and round . . .

"Car in lane four, one hundred and ninety laps. Lane eight, one hundred seventy-nine.

Lane seven, one hundred eighty. Lane six, one hundred sixty-two. Lane five, one hundred seventy-eight. Lane three," Chick listened hard, "one hundred eighty."

He was tied with Jack! He didn't listen any further. *Come on, Stingie! Come on!*

He was even with Jack's Chaparral coming down the sweeper and along the straightaway. At the first hairpin Jack edged by him. He held the lead going to the second curve. At the underpass the Stingray caught up and stayed even with the Chaparrel going down the straightaway to the sweeper. Coming down the stretch the Stingray gained a half a section! By the time it was on the top straightaway again it was two sections ahead!

Round and round . . .

"One hundred ninety-nine! TWO HUNDRED!"

The Main Event was over.

Chick laid the controller aside and stretched his aching fingers and thumb.

"The winner! Lane four, Frank Spry!

Second prize winner, lane three, Chick Grover!" That's all he wanted to know. He didn't
listen any further.

Ken Jason and Butch Slade slapped him
heartily on the back. "Nice going, Chick!"
they cried enthusiastically.

"Thanks, guys," he said shakily.

A hand grabbed his and shook it hard. Jack
Harmon wore a smile a mile wide. "Congratulations, Chick! You were great!"

His heart was pumping. He was trembling
all over. He felt great.

"Thanks, Jack. How — how did you do?"

"Didn't you hear? I came in third."

"Guess we both have a couple of hot
bombs."

"It's not only the bombs," said Jack. "Well,
I don't want to sound like a braggart, but it's
the man at the controllers too. You have a
smart thumb, Chick. And most important of
all you didn't get rattled."

"I would've lost if I had," said Chick. "You
knew it, too."

"Yes, I did." Jack shrugged. "I'm sorry about that. I hope you believe me."

"I do."

Chick was given a gold ribbon and a five-dollar gift certificate entitling him to purchase merchandise at *Mort's Pit Stop*. Jack was given a blue ribbon with a two-dollar gift certificate.

Chick thought a while, then held the envelope containing the gift certificate to Ken. "Here, for giving me that Stingray body."

Ken's eyes popped. "You crazy? You earned it! It's yours!"

"But you gave me the body. And you never took a cent for it. Please, Ken, take it."

Ken pushed it away. "Not on your life. You fixed up the Stingray from scratch. You deserve every bit of your winnings yourself."

"Boy, have you changed," said Jack. "Like Ken says, keep your winnings. You earned every bit of it."

"Then let's have a team," suggested Chick. "The four of us."

"Now you're talking sense!" Jack exclaimed. "We'll scratch-build models. You can be our chief designer. Okay?"

Chick laughed. "Okay! Great! Let's go home and get started."

Model Racing Car Glossary

chassis: car's frame, suspension system, axles, wheels and tires.

color dots: round dots attached to hood of car to identify its lane.

controller: a plunger (thumb-operated), or a trigger, that supplies power to a slot car's motor.

deslotting: the flag, or guide, leaving the slot, thereby stopping the car.

doughnut: loop on track.

Epoxy: adhesive cement.

ess (or s) bend: S-shaped curve of the track.

flag: guide that fits into slot and steers the car.

frame: the structure of the car that supports the motor, body, suspension system and slot guide.

full throttle point: fast area on track.

goop the tires: running tires over a pad of oil of wintergreen or other additive for traction.

Grand Prix: same as Formula 1. Slim, single-seat, open cockpit cars without fenders.

GT (*Gran Turismo*): Italian for Grand Touring. An enclosed type of racing car.

hot thumb: name given to thumb depressing controller lever.

nerfing: when a car sidewinds at a curve and strikes another car, causing it to leave the track.

race director (*or marshal*): man who starts and directs the race, using a stopwatch for timing. He has complete authority over race events. He arranges the events, appoints the officials and enforces the rules.

spin-out: deslotting of a racing car's flag as car turns a corner at too high a speed.

straight: a straightaway on the track.

sweeper: a wide, sweeping, high-speed turn.

"Thumbs down!": thumb lever is depressed by all participants to start race. When all thumbs are down the director signals "Go!" and either he or the manager turns on the switch.

"Thumbs up!": warning call for beginning of race to insure all thumbs are away from controller for a fair start.

"Track!": call made by race director, or a turn marshal, when a car goes onto another lane, leaps over railing or deslots and hits another car.

turn marshal: man stationed at turns of the raceway during a race. He shouts "Track!" when a car deslots. He then replaces the car on the track, or removes it altogether, depending on the type of race.